Praise for Katriena Knights's
Dealing with David

"I love reading a book like this where I connect with one or both of the main characters. I recommend y'all checking this one out."

~ *Guilty Pleasures Book Reviews*

"*Dealing with David* was an excellent story."

~ *Fallen Angel Reviews*

Look for these titles by *Katriena Knights*

Now Available:

Starchild
Earthchild
Where There's a Will
Necromancing Nim

Dealing with David

Katriena Knights

Wood County Public Library
Bowling Green, Ohio 43402

Samhain Publishing, Ltd.
11821 Mason Montgomery Road, 4B
Cincinnati, OH 45249
www.samhainpublishing.com

Dealing with David
Copyright © 2013 by Katriena Knights
Print ISBN: 978-1-61921-115-5
Digital ISBN: 978-1-60928-773-3

Editing by Linda Ingmanson
Cover by Kendra Egert

This book is a work of fiction. The names, characters, places, and incidents are products of the writer's imagination or have been used fictitiously and arc not to be construed as real. Any resemblance to persons, living or dead, actual events, locale or organizations is entirely coincidental.

All Rights Are Reserved. No part of this book may be used or reproduced in any manner whatsoever without written permission, except in the case of brief quotations embodied in critical articles and reviews.

First Samhain Publishing, Ltd. electronic publication: April 2012
First Samhain Publishing, Ltd. print publication: March 2013

Dedication

For Linda Ingmanson, who made me hammer this into something more than it was before.

Chapter One

Not for the first time, Tony Mullin wondered why in the world she had agreed to stand up in Jim and Julia Richie's second wedding. Looking at herself in the mirror in the dark blue velvet medieval monstrosity of a dress, she couldn't really come up with an answer.

Except that Julia was her best friend, had been since forever, and renewing her vows on her tenth anniversary meant the world to her. Plus—and Tony was hesitant to admit the additional motivation even to herself—a good portion of her high school graduating class was going to be there, as well as Julia's other friends and family. None of Tony's fellow classmates had seen her since not long after graduation. Truth to tell, Tony had something to prove.

With a sigh, Tony adjusted the tall, pointy hat over her sleekly upswept hair and pinned it in place, adjusting the gauzy blue veils around her face. A collection of dark blonde strands refused to stay in place, falling in less than artful disarray around her face. She looked ridiculous.

The fabric was wonderful, though. Tony slid her hand down the sensuous softness of the velvet and imagined once again the suit it would become once the ceremony was over—Tony's own version of a designer suit she'd seen in a fashion magazine. It was one of the reasons she'd finally agreed to participate, especially when Julia had offered to foot the bill.

The dippy hat seemed to sit a bit too low on her forehead. Tony loosened a few pins and readjusted it. It hadn't seemed right, letting Julia buy the dress. But Julia had insisted.

"It's not a *wedding* wedding, after all," she'd argued. "We're just renewing our vows."

Tony had just shaken her head, knowing she was about to agree to whatever Julia asked, as much to get her hands on that rich, blue velvet as anything else. "I still can't believe you convinced Jim to wear tights."

Julia and Jim's first wedding had been a simple affair, with a Justice of the Peace presiding and Tony and her then-husband Rudy James serving as witnesses. But Julia had always wanted a big to-do with the wedding party in medieval garb, and that was what she was about to get. The participants were the same—Julia as bride, Jim as groom and Tony as the lone bridesmaid—but the setting looked like something out of a bad Robin Hood movie.

"More like *Monty Python and the Holy Grail*," Tony muttered. She stepped out to meet the crowd.

Not for the first time, David Peterson wondered why he'd been invited to Julia and Jim Richie's second wedding.

Apparently, he wasn't the only guest with the same question. Except the curious gazes that followed him as he walked up the aisle asked not, "What is *he* doing here?" but "Who *is* he?"

David muffled a smile as he sat down. He had most of a pew to himself. The guest list appeared to consist of his and Julia's entire graduating class, but that had only been about fifty people. Maybe thirty-five of them were here now, sprinkled among faces he didn't recognize who were probably Julia's family. Many of their classmates had moved out of state after graduation. David had planned never to see them again. He wanted to see them now, though. Wanted them to see his success. Petty, he knew, but somewhere inside, he was still the nerdy teenager who'd taken the brunt of far too much harassment. He wasn't proud of it, but there it was.

He smoothed his *Star Wars* tie, straightened his Armani suit jacket and picked up his program. As he glanced over the order of the ceremony, his heart did a strange little flip, and suddenly, he understood why the universe had conspired to put him in the same room with the people who'd ruined his teenage years.

Julia's single bridesmaid was Antonytte Mullin.

Mullin. Not James. Mullin.

And David knew he had fallen into the hands of Fate. The question was, what would he do now he was there?

Tony adjusted her big, pointy hat for the hundredth time while Julia preened soberly, preparing for the first of the guests to reach the short receiving line. The wedding had gone off perfectly and, in spite of its eccentricities, had been kind of beautiful.

Spotting her old cheerleading friends approaching in the line, Tony edged Julia a sidelong glance. "I don't understand why you invited Cheryl and Missy."

Julia had never been fond of the two most popular girls in the school, but Tony's concern was more selfish. She had something to prove, yes, but Cheryl and Missy had been her best friends in high school. She hadn't seen either of them since her divorce, and didn't want to spend the whole evening explaining things to the two friends who'd been most supportive of her dating and eventual marriage to Rudy James.

Julia shrugged. "I thought you might want to see them. I mean, you guys were the tight little cheerleading trio in high school." She readjusted her white velvet bodice, which had been dislodged slightly by the shrug, then smoothed her dark hair, pinned up under her own tall, pointy hat. "A lot of them still live up this way, and God knows they could use a party." She turned to Jim. "Your hose are bagging again, darling."

Jim gave his wife a wry look. "Ask me if I care."

Tony looked down at Jim's wrinkly ankles, grinning. She thought Jim was quite a sport, agreeing to wear the tights and blue velvet tunic. Not to mention the weird little pointy shoes. To be asked to hike up his hose every five minutes was, in Tony's mind and apparently Jim's as well, above and beyond the call of duty.

Then the bride's uncle arrived to clasp Jim's hand warmly and say, "I'll tell you, boy, that was the weirdest damn wedding I've ever been to."

Tony gamely shook hands and accepted pecks on the cheek, all the while feeling her hat edge closer and closer to her eyebrows. There hadn't seemed to be nearly so many guests when they were seated in the church. The line seemed to go on forever.

Then, quite suddenly, time stopped.

He was near the end of the line, and Tony had no idea who he was. Tall and slim, he had dark hair and a wide jaw. His suit fit him too well not to be expensive, and something about the way he held himself, the way he walked, made every hormone in her body stand at attention. At first she thought he might be the spouse of one of her old schoolmates, but he stood between two couples and was unmistakably alone. Maybe he was related to Julia. But something made her think she should know him, a disconcerting tickle in her brain that made her actually try to scratch her head, then stop abruptly when her questing fingers once again encountered the hat.

Tony found herself less and less able to concentrate on what she was doing as he came closer. The tickle continued, but her brain refused to put together the pieces that would identify him. It was as if she could see his true identity out of the corner of her eye but couldn't look directly at it.

Something in her knew him, though. Something that made her heart speed up and her breath catch in the back of her throat. Her hands had gone suddenly damp, and all her ridiculous, quasi-medieval clothes felt too tight. She wanted to rush up to him and demand his name. Or run the other direction and hide behind a handy curtain.

Who the hell *was* he?

His turn came. Julia and Jim greeted him like they knew him but didn't say his name. Then he turned to Tony. Something disturbingly familiar lurked in those gray eyes, but Tony still found herself at a loss.

He squeezed her hand, then leaned forward to put a small kiss on her cheek. Her face started to burn, as if she'd suddenly contracted the flu. Or Ebola, or something else that made her face hot, her hands cold and her throat constrict so that, for a moment, she thought she couldn't breathe. When he drew back, he was smiling.

"Nice hat," he said and went on his way. She watched him go, wishing her heart would slow to its normal pace. She had a feeling it wouldn't until he moved out of eyeshot.

She was right.

Tony finally got permission from Julia to remove her hat for the short drive to the reception, mostly because she couldn't get into the car with it on. When they arrived at the Eagle Creek Community Center, she conveniently forgot it in the back seat.

The drive had been brief but picturesque. Eagle Creek was a small town nestled in a valley between jutting peaks that eventually rose into the Continental Divide. Silver-green aspen trees highlighted the lower flanks of the mountains, the wind making the color shimmer. The community center itself sat in the shadow of a lesser peak and was surrounded by aspens and Ponderosa pines older than God. As Tony slid out of the car, the wind picked up a bit, tossing the aspen leaves around with a sound like flowing water. Under a low, glowering sky that promised an April snow, she dashed hatless into the building.

Julia didn't seem to notice Tony's hat deficiency. In fact, she didn't seem to notice Tony at all as Tony took a seat next to the bride and groom at the head table. They were as absorbed in each other as real newlyweds. Envious, Tony sipped her water and tried to pretend she wasn't a bitter divorcée.

Well, maybe not *that* bitter. Or at least she was trying not to be. But the fact remained that it had only been three years since her divorce, and weddings—even this one—still left a bad taste in her mouth.

Or maybe especially this one. After all, this wasn't a promise between two people to love each other forever, made in the heat of passion. This was an affirmation of a love that had survived ten years and appeared to be stronger than ever. Tony despaired of ever finding such a thing.

Thinking along those lines wasn't going to help her put up the positive front she'd intended, though. To distract herself, she took in the decorations and the reactions of the other guests.

The community center was beautifully decked out with paper lanterns designed to resemble floating candles. It looked like something out of a Harry Potter movie, Tony thought. The tables all had faux velvet runners, and the punch poured in magenta arcs from a silver fountain, where guests caught it with small, pewter steins. Sitting next to the fountain was the wedding cake, designed to look like a castle with a medieval king and queen perched on top. A crepe-paper dragon adorned the dais where the DJ had set up his equipment. Tony smiled. Julia had jumped into the medieval theme in a big way. Good for her.

Oddly, her thoughts suddenly turned to Mr. Mysterious from the reception line. He hadn't arrived yet, as far as she could see. She wanted to be ready for him when he did, although she wasn't certain what being ready for him would entail. She still hadn't quite placed him, although she'd started thinking about algebra for no reason. Maybe it was connected. Maybe she really, really wanted to figure out who the hell the guy was and if she should be embarrassed for not recognizing him right off.

Maybe she was just crazy.

After a few minutes of nuzzling and cooing, Jim was finally distracted by a friend who dropped by to chat, and Julia turned to Tony.

"Sorry about that," she said. "This is our first evening away from the kids in about a year."

"It's okay," Tony replied. She chewed on an ice cube and swallowed it. She usually ate dinner about five-thirty, and it was rapidly approaching six. "Did you notice the clouds?" she asked Julia. "Is it supposed to snow tonight?"

Jim bent his head around to insinuate himself into the conversation. "Yeah, it's supposed to snow, but just a dusting, as far as I could tell from the weather report."

Julia waved her hand, dismissing Jim's statement. "What can you tell from the weather report? They can guess about Denver, but they have no idea what's going to happen up here."

Tony hoped the weather report was right. It was a long drive down the mountain to Lakewood, and if it snowed too much, she'd be stranded—

The thought lurched to a halt. There he was again. Standing in line at the bar. Tony elbowed Julia frantically and probably harder than necessary.

"Ow!" Julia exclaimed. "What's the matter?"

"Who *is* that?" Tony pointed carefully, holding her hand close to the table.

Julia looked toward the bar. "Who is who?"

"The tall one with the brown hair and the expensive suit."

Julia looked, frowning; then suddenly, her eyebrows rose, and a slow smile spread across her face. "You don't recognize him?"

"Should I?"

Julia's smile had become disturbingly sly. "I don't know. Why don't you go get yourself a drink and see if you can find out?"

Tony set her mouth and stood. "Maybe I just will. Would you care for anything?"

"Tom Collins," said Jim, who somehow managed to follow his own conversation yet dip into Julia's at the most opportune moments.

Julia sniffed her opinion of Jim's drink choice. "Traitor. I want a glass of that mead your brother made for me."

Tony grinned. At the risk of further offending Julia, *she* was getting a fuzzy navel.

By the time Tony got in line, two more people stood between her and the mystery man. She watched him as he waited his turn. The woman in front of him, whom Tony recognized from her sophomore biology class, chatted him up shamelessly, eyes wide and flirtatious as she smiled and preened and touched him on the sleeve. A surge of possessiveness hit Tony from left field. What the hell was that about? She'd never felt possessive about a man. Not even her ex-husband, although by the time they'd split up, she'd felt more like kicking him out of her car than actively claiming him as hers. But the girl flirting with Mr. Mysterious? Tony wanted to slap her, or at the very least push her out of the way so Tony could brush the lint off the man's sleeve herself.

Instead, she gathered her velvet train closer to keep it from being stepped on and examined the man in question. Mostly she could just see the back of his head, but occasionally he turned enough to expose his profile. His nose was long and straight—almost too long, really—and his dark forelock hung down across his forehead. There *was* something familiar about him, but she couldn't place it. It was like seeing something out of the corner of her eye, but when she tried to look directly at him, it slipped out of her sight.

And her timing couldn't have been worse. He got his drink and left the bar, and Tony still had to wait her turn. By the time she had acquired her collection of drinks from a bartender wearing a long, red tunic and a jaunty hat with a feather in it, the mystery man had disappeared into the crowd milling toward the hors d'oeuvres.

Irritated but undaunted, Tony inched her way back to her table, scanning the crowd as she did so. She squinted over her shoulder at a brown-haired man across the room and had just determined he wasn't her quarry when she crashed full-tilt into a wide chest. Mead, orange juice, schnapps, and whatever was in a Tom Collins went everywhere.

Tony swung around, her face going hot. "I'm so sorry," she said. "I'm so, so sorry—"

And then she stopped. Because the chest she'd collided with belonged to *him*, and some strange quirk inside her head had finally sorted out the off-kilter algebra connection and figured out who he was.

"Oh my God," she said, vaguely aware of Julia heading toward them with piles of napkins, more aware of the gray eyes looking down at her, of the big hands held slightly aloft while liquor dripped from their fingertips. "Oh my God," she said again. "David Peterson?"

"Hi, Tony," he said brightly. "What happened to your hat?"

The look of utter bafflement on Tony's face couldn't have pleased David more. He had her at a disadvantage for a change. With a nod, he took a handful of napkins from Julia. Julia poked Tony, who took her own supply of napkins and handed over the nearly empty trio of glasses in exchange.

"I'm so sorry," Tony repeated. She separated one of the napkins and began to press it against the lapels of David's jacket. David wiped his hands and wished she'd spilled onto his pants.

"It's okay," he said. "It really is."

"But this suit looks expensive. I hope it doesn't stain—" She broke off as David grasped both her wrists in his hands, pulling her away just as she started to delve under the jacket to daub at his shirt. He just couldn't take it anymore.

"I have a really good dry cleaner," he said. "Don't worry about it."

She drew her hands back to herself, her forehead creased in an endearing frown. Looking into his face, she blinked twice, then said, "Send me the bill."

"I said it's okay. Honest." He smiled then, and she smiled back tentatively as if she hadn't ever met him. She was as beautiful as he remembered—more so, since the intervening years had been kind to her. Her honey-blonde hair fell in waves to her shoulders, no longer confined by the pointy hat, and the medieval gown, although awkward and not the best fit, still managed to accentuate her curves and the sleek lines of her body. Of course, she was one of those women who would look perfect in nothing but a ratty T-shirt and worn jeans.

Maybe he was prejudiced. He'd have to keep an eye on these involuntary reactions. He'd learned to control his emotions in the course of becoming who he now was, and he wouldn't let even Tony pull him off-kilter that way.

Still, she was beautiful. On a whim, he crooked one damp elbow toward her. "May I escort you to your seat?"

A moment passed; then Tony slid her arm through the bend of his elbow. As she moved into step next to him, he thanked God once again for whatever urge had made him show up today. He had no desire anymore to impress his classmates. He only wanted to find out what was going on with Tony. He'd find out where her life stood now, and then he'd come up with a plan to put himself in her way for a while, to see what happened. He had to try, at least. He hadn't gotten where he was today by squandering opportunities.

He mentally thanked Julia as he caught her broad grin. He wasn't certain exactly what she had up her sleeve, but he was willing to go with the flow as long at it got him closer to what he wanted.

"Why don't you sit with us for a bit, David?" Julia suggested as David tucked Tony's chair under her. "I'd like to hear what you've been up to lately."

"I can't sit here," David protested. "This is the bride's table."

"Oh, please. It's my wedding—you'll sit wherever I tell you to. Sit your fanny down."

David acquiesced with a mock-sober nod. He hadn't seen Julia in a long time, and he'd forgotten how ebullient she could be. No wonder she'd been friends with literally everybody in their tiny high school.

He looked at Tony and decided she didn't seem too averse to Julia's suggestion. Another happy coincidence, or maybe Fate was still dragging him along for the ride. Either way, he wasn't going to fight the order when it was exactly what he wanted to do, anyway. Pulling up an empty chair from a neighboring table, he sat down.

Tony watched him as he settled next to her. Up close, he was starting to look more familiar. She remembered the short, brown hair and gray eyes. But no glasses obscured those eyes today, and where there had once been a mass of silver in his mouth, now there was a spectacular set of even, white teeth. He was still tall but lanky, not gangly. His mouth, also changed by the absence of braces, curved with undeniable sensuality. Tony found herself wishing he would smile, and he did, beautifully.

"You look exactly the way I remember you," he said.

"You...don't," she managed, then mentally smacked herself. That hadn't come out right at all.

The smile turned rueful. "I've been getting a lot of that."

Julia patted Tony's shoulder. "I'm going to go get some new drinks."

"Great. Thanks." Then Tony realized that left her alone with David. She composed herself and turned back toward him.

She took a moment to adjust, studying him, trying to make the changed features look right. In the process, she noticed a wet spot on his white shirt where she'd caught him with her drink. Next to it hung a brightly colored tie with little pictures of R2D2 all over it.

"Nice tie," she said.

"I want to be R2D2 when I grow up," he said, then, "I hear you're living in Lakewood."

"Can't we talk about you?" She tried to make it sound coquettish and failed miserably. At the same time, she wondered why his interest made her uncomfortable. She'd come here wanting to prove she was doing fine on her own. Now she suddenly felt like she had nothing to brag about and more to be ashamed of. She wasn't going to impress David wearing a dippy medieval gown while talking about her ugly divorce and her current lack of permanent employment. And suddenly, unaccountably, she did want to impress him.

David shrugged. "I was curious, is all. I haven't seen you in ages. And I have an office in Lakewood. That's why I asked."

An office? The question begged asking, but Tony didn't ask it. She decided instead to satisfy his curiosity, just to see what he might say. "I moved down there after the divorce."

David looked down at the table, suddenly far too interested in straightening the napkins. Tony found herself holding her breath. What would he say? More importantly, what was he thinking? Was it too much to hope he was happy she was single again? Was she a complete idiot thinking that, or just letting the wedding vibe rub off on her?

He looked back at her, and she met his gaze full on, letting it soak into her. She still couldn't reconcile this handsome man with the geeky social disaster he'd been in high school. And he had beautiful eyes. She'd never really gotten a chance to see them through the thick glasses he'd worn in high school. He didn't appear to be wearing contacts, either.

"I'm sorry to hear that." His voice was careful and quiet, his face soft with genuine sympathy.

Tony casually waved it off, but her fingers trembled a little.

"It's been a few years. I'm better off without him." True, but that hadn't made the transition any easier. Only a few years, yes, but they'd been hard ones.

David nodded. "So what are you doing now?"

Tony straightened, reminding herself she should be proud of her accomplishments, not worried about what anyone might think. "I'm taking classes at Red Rocks Community College, and I'm working as a temp. Clerical stuff mostly. I had a permanent job for about a year, but with the classes, temping worked better." There. She'd made good decisions—decisions that had worked for her. She was happy about that. Proud.

Even so, her brain clicked into defensive mode, ready for the vague smirk, the condescension. She'd always gotten that from Rudy, no matter what she tried to pursue. Or it had seemed that way to her.

She didn't get it from David. "That's great!" he said with genuine enthusiasm. "What are you taking?"

"Accounting."

"Really?" He seemed surprised, then disappointed. "I always thought you'd study art."

"There's no money in an art degree," she countered too sharply. "What would I do with it?"

"My company is always looking for artists. Of course, computer knowledge is good too. Not necessarily programming, but if you can use graphics software, you're a few steps ahead of the game."

Tony looked away, the eye contact more than she could handle. "I tried the art thing. It didn't work." End of story, as far as she was concerned.

She didn't want him to talk to her about her art anymore. Her hands clenched on the table, she waited for him to push the issue. But he just looked at her, and suddenly she felt like he could see right into her.

"Do you like the classes you're taking?" he said.

Tony shrugged. "They're okay."

He started to say something else, but Julia breezed up, carrying a drink in each hand.

"Here you are, Tony. Fresh drink. You and David getting reacquainted?"

David looked at Tony, fingering the sweating surface of his glass. "Yeah."

Julia looked from one to the other. Tony tried to relax. What did it matter what David thought about her, anyway? She was getting along just fine on her own. But the knot in her stomach made her feel like she'd screwed something up, and she didn't even know what.

"Well," said Julia as if nothing were amiss, "now it's time for *my* interrogation, David. What have you been up to lately?"

"Let's see. I went to MIT, and I almost got a PhD; then a college buddy of mine called me up one day and asked if I'd be interested in helping him out with some game software. One thing led to another, and now we own our own company."

Tony's eyes widened. Good grief! Not only had he grown up handsome, but it sounded like he was rich as well. David nudged her gently.

"Maybe you've heard of Tachyon Software?"

Tony shook her head. "No, sorry."

"Then maybe you've heard of *Dark Princes*."

"Oh, yeah!" Julia chimed in. "My seven-year-old loves that game. I bribe him with it to do his homework." She shook her head in amazement. "Your company produced that?"

"That's right. If you read the credits—and I know nobody ever does—my name's in there a few times."

"Wow. You must have made a mint."

David nodded. "It's been fairly lucrative. In fact, we're working on expanding because of that game's success. We're starting up an educational division. Plus *Dark Princes II* will be out May first, and *Dark Princes III* is under production."

They talked on. Tony tuned them out, her throat gone dry with nerves. There was no point telling David any more about her life. He'd been so successful, and she'd turned everything she'd touched to mud. Absently, she pulled a pen from her little sequined purse and began to sketch on the napkins.

Dinner arrived eventually. Fortunately, Julia—or maybe it was Jim—had decided not to carry the medieval theme through into dinner, so nobody had to eat with their fingers.

David and Julia continued to talk, finally enticing Jim to join them in discussing tomorrow's Avalanche game. Tony picked at her chicken and made a passable miniature mountain range out of her mashed potatoes. She wished she could be somewhere else. Anywhere else, as long as David wasn't sitting next to her being successful and rich and ridiculously handsome.

It seemed like everyone she'd gone to school with was in a better position than she was. Happier, still married, raising children, programming world-famous video games. She was studying accounting and typing forms for companies she rarely stayed with more than a week. She had a new assignment Monday, in fact—the previous job had ended on Thursday. They just didn't need her anymore. Nobody really needed her anymore. She didn't even have a dog, for Pete's sake. Before she'd come here, she'd framed that differently. She was free and living her own life, doing what she'd decided to do. Now it all just seemed kind of pathetic.

When dessert arrived—generous chunks of the castle-shaped wedding cake—David tried to pull her back into conversation.

"Good cake, isn't it?"

"Yes, it's good," Tony agreed briefly.

David studied her as if planning his next step. Tony fought not to squirm under his scrutiny.

"So," he said finally, "do you still paint?"

Tony squashed a small piece of cake with her fork. "Not really. I do some sketching and the occasional watercolor. And I sew, which doesn't sound artistic, but it is."

David nodded soberly, looking at the scribbled-upon paper napkins piled haphazardly next to her plate. Tony suppressed an urge to snatch them up and hide them under the table. They suddenly seemed far too personal, almost like he was looking at her naked.

"It's nice you haven't dropped it altogether," David said. "I always thought you were really talented."

"Thanks," Tony mumbled.

She turned her attention to her cake. Why was he so interested in her art? Sure, maybe once she'd dreamed of running off to Paris and painting future masterpieces, but that had been an adolescent fantasy. There was no room for that kind of silliness in the grown-up world. Even commercial art was a difficult and competitive field. She'd never make it anywhere without a Bachelor's degree or, better yet, a Master's, and that wasn't happening any time soon. Best to let that dream fall to the side where it belonged.

She could feel Julia looking at her again. Wondering, no doubt, why Tony was being so prickly. Tony was beginning to wonder herself. Crankiness didn't become her. Suddenly, she felt like she couldn't stay at the table for another minute. She picked up her empty glass.

"I'll be right back," she said. Only after she'd left the table did she realize it had been rude to go get herself another drink without offering to get anyone else one.

"Blast him, anyway," she said to herself, straightening her dress as she crossed to the bar. "Nobody should be that good-looking." Especially not David Peterson. He should still be skinny and ugly, damn him. Why hadn't she been offered some chrysalis she could crawl into and come out perfect like he had?

She ordered a Bailey's Irish Crème from the bartender in hopes it would calm her down. She needed to get herself under control if she was going to be stuck for the rest of the evening with David. And the person she was turning into in his presence wasn't a person she was proud of.

When she came back, though, he was gone. Off to chat with some other acquaintances, Julia told her. Tony sat and finished her cake in some semblance of peace.

"Pretty amazing, huh?" said Julia. "Who'd've dreamed David Peterson would end up not only good-looking but filthy rich?"

"Yeah, and I'm still typing memos."

"Is that what's bothering you?" Julia's voice sounded careful, almost hesitant.

Tony turned to Julia, only then realizing how bitter and glum she'd sounded. "David owns his own company, Cheryl's husband works for the governor, you've got Jim and three really cute kids, and I'm just a divorced temp with no money and a student loan. And it's not even real college." She pushed her hand through her hair, trying to compose herself. "Why should that bother me?"

Julia patted her shoulder reassuringly. "I think you're recovering nicely." She took a drink, only partially hiding her mischievous smile. "And I think David still likes you."

Tony waved the comment off. "Still? He never liked me to begin with." If he had, it had probably just been a high school infatuation, and Tony had no interest in that. Infatuation was what had brought her into Rudy's orbit and kept her there far too long.

Julia shook her head and started to say something, but just then the room filled with music. Tony looked up to see the DJ getting his equipment fired up from the dais at the front of the room. Julia, grinning, turned to her husband.

"Let's dance." She swept him away, leaving Tony alone at the table, but not before she leaned down to Tony. "We'll discuss your low self-esteem later, missy. I don't like seeing you beat yourself up."

Tony nodded, but she wasn't looking forward to Julia's post mortem of Tony's newly crappy mood. David had left half his cake, she noticed. She looked surreptitiously around, then proceeded to eat it. Cake helped everything. Especially when it had cream cheese frosting.

When that was gone, she picked up her pen again. A few minutes later, she realized she'd sketched her ex, Rudy. She tore the napkin into a collection of tiny shreds and dropped them into her leftover coffee. Then she stole David's napkin and started drawing again.

The sketching relaxed her, and she had just about decided to get up and try to mingle when a hand touched her shoulder. Shock filled her again, though milder this time, as she looked up into David's much-changed face. God, he was gorgeous. Her mopeyness slid down a few notches as her primal responses took over again. He made her body thrum like a banjo. Or maybe something a little less twangy.

"Would you like to dance?" he asked.

Tony considered. There could be no harm in it. The DJ was playing fast tunes, so she wouldn't have to deal with the awkwardness of dancing close. Besides, she needed to have some fun or this whole evening was going to be a disaster.

"Okay. What the hell?" She stood and let him lead her onto the dance floor.

Tony really had no clue how to dance properly, but everyone else was just wiggling in rhythm, so she followed suit. David moved a bit more gracefully. He had definitely grown into his height. In high school, he'd been a beanpole with legs. He still had long legs, but the rest of him matched up better. He was tall, lean and lanky, and filled his suit nicely. Big feet too, Tony noticed, then mentally slapped herself when she found herself wondering if big feet really did mean big other things.

After a moment, David danced closer. "My cake disappeared!" He had to shout over the music. "Would you know anything about that?"

"Mice!" Tony shouted back. "Really big mice!" She held her hands about three feet apart to demonstrate.

David grinned. Tony's heart bounced in her chest, and it had nothing to do with the exertion of dancing. The grin made him look about sixteen, but it was a sixteen from an alternate reality where he'd been sinfully cute instead of gangly and awkward. The music faded, and he stepped even closer.

"I think it was a little blonde mouse named Tony."

"Well, one of them was kind of light brown, but I didn't ask its name." The repartee lifted her spirits. He really was kind of fun to be around when she wasn't drowning herself in her own glum.

In the background, the DJ bantered. Tony didn't register what he was saying. A few more couples joined the group on the dance floor.

"Not that it matters," David went on. "I wasn't that hungry anyway."

The music started again. "Unchained Melody," by the Righteous Brothers. Tony felt a lurch of panic. Trust the DJ to pick now to play a love song. Her brain scrambled for a gracious excuse to bow out. Before she could draw anything but a blank, David scooped her into his arms.

Chapter Two

For a second, she stood still, staring up at him. The length of his body pressed against hers, solid and warm. One big hand cupped her waist; the other tangled through her fingers. This close, she had little choice but to look right up into his gray eyes. He was smiling, a soft curve of that sinfully sensual mouth. She had a sudden urge to touch his lips.

"I'm not going to bite, Tony," he said. Far from reassured, and wondering uncomfortably if she might enjoy it if he bit her, Tony settled her arm around him and let him lead her into the dance.

Tony hadn't danced like this in a long time. Not since well before her divorce. Rudy had never been much for dancing. She'd never responded quite this way to Rudy, either. She couldn't even think tucked up to David like this. They fit together remarkably well, especially considering he was a good eight inches taller than she was. All sense seemed to have been driven from her head so that her conscious mind could fill totally with the warmth and shape of his body, the texture of his palm against hers. Even the smell of him overwhelmed her, subtle as it was. No cologne, just a spicy odor of soap and skin.

"So…" she said, trying to string a few words together in her head. "Where are you living these days?"

"I just bought a house not far from here." His voice was far too close to her ear; his breath stirred her hair, setting off a chain reaction of unruly hormones that made it hard to concentrate. "I was in Denver for quite a while until we got the office established."

"Why didn't you set up business on the East Coast, since you went to college there?"

"Didn't want to. This is really a great location. California and New York are too crowded, but this is just about right." He bent away from her a bit, looking down into her face. "And it's home."

Tony swallowed. He was just too hot, too close and too handsome. He smiled. His dark hair had fallen forward onto his forehead. A slight sheen of sweat glazed his upper lip. She wanted to lick it.

To her increased discomfort, Tony found herself wondering if he looked like this right after he made love. The image captured her, as did the depths of his gray eyes. She stared at him, not even sure she was dancing anymore, as the song wound down around them. She could feel his heartbeat against her chest, and his body moved beneath her arm as he breathed.

"Tony?"

She jumped out of David's arms and nearly out of her own skin as Julia touched her shoulder. Whatever spell David's presence had cast over her fell in pieces at her feet. She turned toward Julia, trying to pretend she hadn't just nearly suffered a heart attack. She wasn't entirely sure she hadn't wet herself.

Julia didn't seem to have noticed, in any case. "Tony, I'm sorry to interrupt, but I need to ask you a really big favor."

The concern on Julia's face made Tony reach out to grasp her arm, startlement forgotten. "What's wrong? Are you all right?"

Julia waved it off with a flap of her hand, but Tony could tell she was concerned. "The babysitter called—the baby has a fever. Most likely it's nothing, but I said we'd come on home."

"I hope she's okay."

"She'll be fine, I'm sure. There's been a cold going around at day care." She took Tony's hand. "I'm really sorry I have to ask you this, but could you stay and be sure things get cleaned up and give the checks to the DJ and the bartender?"

"Of course. Go right home and don't even worry about it."

Julia's fingers tightened. "Thank you so much. I owe you one."

"It's okay, really. Give me a call tomorrow and let me know how things are."

She watched Julia go, then turned back toward David. He frowned after Julia but shifted his attention to Tony as she met his gaze.

"Let me know if I can help."

Tony nodded, grateful for the offer. She wasn't sure she wanted to end up alone in the community center with him, though. Things could happen. Bad, sticky things that would be hard to take back. Especially if they kept drinking. She made a silent vow to stay away from the bar for the rest of the evening.

"Thanks," she told him. "I don't think we really have to do anything for a while, though."

"Just let me know."

The DJ started another slow song, and David spread his arms, inviting her back in. Tony twisted her hands together. She was a coward, she knew it, and she wasn't afraid to take the coward's way out.

"I'll be right back," she said. "I have to go to the ladies' room."

Dealing with David

As luck would have it, Cheryl was in the ladies' room, chatting with Missy, another member of the old cheerleading squad. Cheryl, whose husband now worked for the governor. Cheryl, who still had perfect auburn hair and a figure most women would kill for. And who could actually walk in six-inch heels, a talent Tony had never mastered. Missy was still similarly gorgeous. They'd been tight in high school—best friends—but in retrospect, Tony thought the only thing that had really glued them together had been their mutual involvement in the cheerleading squad.

"Oh, yes," Cheryl was saying. "All three networks are jockeying for an interview with Bob—" She broke off, seeing Tony in the mirror. "Oh, hi, Tony." Her expression made Tony think she was miffed to have been interrupted.

"Hello, Cheryl. Hi, Missy."

"Hi, Tony!" Missy scampered over for a hug. She seemed a little uncomfortable too, or was that Tony's imagination? No, that hug was too tight. She got the impression Missy was relieved to have been rescued from Cheryl's monologue about her husband and the governor. "How are you? How's Rudy?"

Tony tried very hard to keep her voice neutral. "I have no idea. I haven't spoken to Rudy in three years."

Missy's eyes widened. "Oh, I'm sorry. That must be rough." She laid a hand against her breast in a gesture of concern. Unfortunately, the gesture displayed her three- or four-carat diamond engagement ring and the matching, diamond-studded wedding band to great effect, as if she'd planned it that way.

"I'm getting by," Tony said, absolutely refusing to comment on the garish hunk of squashed carbon. Missy probably hadn't meant anything by it. She was just...flamboyant.

Cheryl smiled knowingly. "Well, it looks like you've got a good chance with the richest man in our graduating class. As infatuated as David was with you in high school, it shouldn't take much for you to get into his wallet."

Tony blinked. There it was again—that comment that David had been infatuated with her in high school. Where was that coming from? Then, realizing what else Cheryl had said, Tony bristled. A moment later, she realized Cheryl had had no intention of being insulting. She was just being Cheryl. "He's changed a lot," she said finally. Then, not quite under her breath, she added, "You haven't."

Cheryl opened her mouth, a shocked look on her face, but before she could say anything, another woman breezed in.

"It's really snowing out there," she announced. "All of you guys are driving down to Denver, right? You might want to take a look."

"Oh, wonderful." Tony headed for the door, relieved to remove herself from the aftermath of her own too-quick mouth.

A few minutes later, she stood outside the front door, watching the snow. There was a good three inches on the ground already, and a gusty wind blew it up in gauzy sheets as more came down. The fall was so thick Tony could barely see across the small parking lot.

"It figures," she said to no one in particular.

The man next to her, who had come out for a cigarette, nodded. "Only in Colorado."

Tony went back inside. The DJ had paused for a drink break, so she went to the booth and picked up the microphone.

"Attention! Listen up, everybody." As if anybody could have missed her impromptu announcement—the ear-bloodying squeal of feedback brought the entire room to attention. Tony shifted the microphone and waved sheepishly. "Sorry. Um...there's been an unexpected development, and the bride and groom had to go home early. Also, there's a big snowstorm brewing outside, so we're going to officially close down the proceedings as of now. Thanks, everybody, for coming."

She passed the checks to the DJ and the bartender, then went to the bride's table. She really wanted to head out and try to beat the worst of the storm, but per her promise to Julia, she had to wait for the other guests to leave so she could be sure things were cleaned up.

David appeared at her elbow as she came down from the DJ booth.

"I'll stick around until you're ready to leave," he told her

"You don't need to do that," she protested. It was sweet of him to offer, but she really didn't need him lurking around like some hunky babysitter. Especially the hunky part. His hotness was just deadly.

"Yes, I do."

Tony opened her mouth to protest again, and he laid a finger on her lips. "Don't argue with me. I'm a CEO—I'm used to having my own way."

She shifted, turning her face away from his touch and stiffening automatically at his words. Then she recognized her own prickle and backed off. He hadn't even sounded bossy. *Stupid brain. He's not Rudy.* "Thanks for the offer, David, but I think I can handle it myself."

He shrugged. "Okay." He pulled his wallet from his hip pocket and extracted a pale blue business card. "Here's my office number. Give me a call. Maybe we can get together for lunch."

"Sure." Tony took the card. Easy enough to lose it, she thought, and avoid the whole issue, but she tucked it carefully into her purse. "I'll talk to you later, then."

"Drive carefully."

She watched him head toward the front door, stopping halfway there to chat with someone she recognized from the old football team. Her gaze didn't seem to want to leave him; she shook her head and forced her attention to her newfound duties.

Picking up his coat from the racks by the front doors, David watched Tony as she passed from table to table, making sure dirty dishes were stacked and ready to be picked up, pausing occasionally for conversation and good-byes.

She'd changed. There had always been a shadow under her perky blonde exterior, the result of a broken family, but now the shadow seemed darker. The faint lines around her eyes and mouth didn't look like they'd been put there by laughter. And she seemed leery of everyone and everything. Even now, smiling and shaking hands with the guests, she didn't seem comfortable with the casual intimacy.

He realized, with some amusement, that he was admiring her from afar, as he'd always done. It was time to change that. And the more he saw of the invisible walls she'd put up around herself, the more he wanted to find his way through them.

He picked up his coat and shrugged it on. He didn't care what she'd said; he wasn't leaving her alone in this weather. Call it his own version of chivalry, but the prince in the Armani suit didn't leave the princess of the discarded big, pointy hat to fend for herself against a surprise Colorado mountain snowstorm.

Not in his world, anyway. He went out to the parking lot to warm up his Jeep.

The snow hadn't let up—not that Tony had expected it to in forty-five minutes. The wind seemed brisker, though, and tiny, icy snowflakes scoured her face as she waded through the snow to her car. They were solid enough to make a *shhh* sound as they struck the cars around her, and the wind made a strange howl that sounded close and distance at the same time. The dress's train dragged in the snow in spite of her best efforts to keep it off the ground, and her shoes were full of slush by the time she reached her car. The parking lot was empty now except for a lone Jeep Cherokee with the engine running. She gave it a cursory glance—someone sat in the driver's seat, probably waiting for the heater to kick in.

Pulling her hand inside her coat sleeve, Tony gripped the edge and used it to brush snow from her driver's side door and window. She'd get the car started first, then clean it off.

Her toes were freezing. She kicked off one snow-filled pump and settled her nylon-clad toes on the accelerator as she turned the key in the ignition.

Nothing.

"What the...?" She turned the key again. Absolutely nothing. The car was dead as a...well, dead as something really, really dead that she couldn't think of right now. She banged on the steering wheel and said something very unladylike. Then, just to be sure, she turned the key again.

This was pointless. She'd have to call the auto club. It was the battery, she was certain. The mechanic had told her it was due to be replaced last time she'd taken the car in for service, but she'd opted to save herself the money and deal with it later. Why did later always have to be so inconvenient?

She pulled out her cell phone. The triangular icon that indicated connection strength was empty. Dammit. Wasn't there a tower nearby? Or was the storm blocking the signal? It was probably her provider—half the time the providers with the best connection down the hill had terrible service in the mountains, and vice versa.

Well, nothing for it but to head back into the community center. Surely there was a phone in there somewhere.

Her footsteps echoed in the deserted room as she made her way to the office area. Maybe she should have let David stay after all. She'd never expected to get stranded. In a pinch, she could call Julia, but even she lived nearly fifteen miles away, and in this weather, on the winding, mountainous roads, it could literally take hours to travel that distance.

She'd dumped the snow out of her shoes, but her feet were still painfully cold. She rubbed her toes against her calf while she dialed the auto club's toll-free number.

A few minutes later, she slammed the phone down and said something even more unladylike.

"What's up?"

Tony nearly jumped out of her own skin. David. Of course. Tony turned around to face him. He must have been the one sitting in the Jeep. As her heart settled back into a normal rhythm, Tony found herself grateful but still annoyed.

"My car's dead," she said. "That was the auto club. The closest affiliated garage is in Buena Vista, and they're so backed up with the weather, they won't be able to help me until morning."

David put a comforting hand on her shoulder. "Don't worry about it. I'll jump it. Just give me the keys. We'll have you out of here in no time."

Tony bristled automatically. "I'm perfectly capable of jumpstarting my own car, thank you very much." Men. They always wanted to take over. And she'd vowed the day she'd signed her divorce papers that she wasn't going to let another one do that to her.

"Then why did you call the auto club?"

He seemed immune to her snarliness, and the amused expression on his face made her feel better instead of worse. He wasn't mocking her. "Well...because I didn't know you were here, duh."

He put his hand out. "The keys, Tony." She looked down at them, still there in her hand. "It's okay to let me help you. Really it is. Have a seat and let your feet warm up. I don't want you losing any toes over a dead battery."

"All right." She handed him the keys. "But I owe you one. And don't think I won't make you collect."

Too late, she realized what she'd said. Her eyes widened, and she stiffened, waiting for David to take advantage of the opening she'd given him.

He closed his hand over the keys and said, "Too easy. Get back to me when you need a more clever and challenging comeback." Then he smiled, both his expression and his tone soft as he added, "Go sit down and find some napkins to draw on. I'll be back in a few."

Watching him depart, Tony shook her head, caught between annoyance, relief and something else she couldn't pin down. Find some napkins to draw on. He knew her too damn well.

Tony pulled a folding chair out of the rack, set it up next to a nearby table and sat on her frozen feet. When she found herself reaching for the pen and extra napkins in her purse, she stopped herself and folded both hands in front of her instead. She'd find something else to do, just to show David he didn't know everything about her anymore. If he ever had, which he hadn't, because they hadn't even known each other that well, and what the hell was going on with everybody thinking he'd been infatuated with her, and—

David returned with a slam of the front door, brushing snow from his coat. By his expression, Tony judged the news was not good.

"Is it running?" she asked.

David shook his head. "I'm sorry, Tony. That battery is really, extremely dead. It looks like your alternator's shot."

Tony's heart sank. "Great. Just great." She pushed her hand through her hair, trying to resign herself. "What am I going to do now?" It was nearly an hour drive back down to Lakewood—definitely longer given the weather.

"I have a guest room," David said. "You're welcome to use it."

Tony sighed. It appeared she had little choice. Eagle Creek wasn't exactly the hotel capital of Colorado, Julia was too far away, and Tony really didn't want to sleep on the floor of the community center.

"All right," she said. "Thanks for the offer."

He shrugged. "Not a problem. Let's lock back up and we'll go. It's not a long drive, but a couple of the roads can be tricky in weather like this." He hesitated. "Good thing my car takes so damn long to warm up."

She wasn't sure she believed that story, but she decided to give him the benefit of the doubt for a change.

Outside, the snow had accumulated to over a foot. David looked at Tony's feet in her damp pumps.

"Not exactly snowshoes, are they?" he said, and before she could protest, he bent and picked her up. Tony drew a startled breath.

"David, put me down."

He stepped out into the snow, holding her tight against his chest. She would have struggled, but she didn't want to end up facedown in the snow. And, truth to tell, his domineering side was making her a bit breathless. It was the type of domineering that made her feel protected instead of belittled. It threw her off balance.

David shook his head. "Sorry. I'll give you my guest room for the night, but I will not take you to the hospital to have your toes amputated."

"I don't think I'm going to get frostbite walking a few yards through a few inches of snow."

"No point taking chances."

It was no use. He was bigger than she was and stronger than his slim build indicated. To make matters worse, she actually felt good cradled against his chest. The snow battered her face, and she bent closer, using his body as a shield.

It was a short trip to his car. When they reached it, he directed her to open the unlocked passenger door, then deposited her inside. He turned on the heat full blast, and a few minutes later, windshields clear and wipers going, they were off.

Watching out the window made her nervous. The snowflakes flying straight at the car turned the headlights into more of a liability than a help, and she found herself tensing, pressing on brakes that didn't exist on her side of the car. She turned her attention to David instead.

His gaze was riveted to the road, hands tight on the steering wheel but not so tight that she got the impression he was anxious. He seemed centered and confident, in control.

To her surprise, she felt her body loosening, relaxing into the embrace of the car's seat. Maybe it wouldn't be so bad to have someone to take care of her if it always felt like this.

She closed her eyes and let her head fall back against the headrest, turning everything over to David.

It felt good, but she knew better than to trust that feeling. She knew it led nowhere she wanted to be.

She didn't open her eyes again until they pulled into the driveway, which was precariously angled and narrow. The snow was nearly two feet deep here, but the Jeep plowed through with aplomb. David pressed the garage door opener. It was hard to see the house in the dark and through the snow, but from the vague, dark bulk, Tony judged it to be fairly large. The garage was big enough for three cars, but only one other occupied the space—a new Mercedes convertible.

"Nice car," Tony said, nodding toward the convertible.

David shrugged. "I like it. It's fun when the weather's nice. Impractical otherwise, though." He shut down the ignition. "Let's get inside and get you warmed up."

Why he would think she was cold, Tony didn't know, unless it had something to do with the way she'd sat huddled and shaking under her inadequate coat all the way home. Just uncurling to get out of the car sent her into a fit of shivers. The car had been relatively warm, but her feet were still cold, and it made the rest of her feel like she was encased in ice.

"I wish I'd known the weather was going to be nasty," she said as she followed David to the door. "I would have brought a heavier coat and some boots."

David pushed the door open and stepped inside, flipping a light switch. "It was supposed to snow, but not like this. I think this one even caught the weathermen by surprise."

"Probably hit the mountains just the right way." Weather always made for good small talk, especially in Colorado where it was so unpredictable and complicated. "I bet there's no snow at all back in Lakewood."

She followed him into a large, one-room lower level. It managed to be utilitarian and smartly decorated at the same time, with medium-gray carpet and black furniture. An entertainment center and a rack of maybe five hundred CDs and another set of shelves full of vinyl records dominated one side of the room. Obviously, he'd been a music fan long before the age of the music download. At a glance, Tony saw everything from Abba to Mozart to ZZ Top. A black leather sectional couch sat strategically among an array of state-of-the-art surround-sound speakers. On the other side of the room was a long, black desk with two computer monitors. CPUs sat on the floor beneath. Two printers occupied another table, and a large drafting table filled the opposite corner. The whole place smelled of new carpeting.

"Office away from office," David said. "I bring programming teams up here to work sometimes. It's a different atmosphere, and things come together sometimes that seemed to be stalled." He turned toward the staircase. "Plus I can play *Dark Princes* and *Dark Princes II* at the same time."

He grinned, and Tony answered it hesitantly. Still a geek at heart, she thought, but these days, there was money in it.

A lot of money, as was demonstrated by the upper level of his house. The place wasn't huge, but it wasn't small, either. Kitchen and living area merged into an airy great room dominated by a huge, moss-rock fireplace. A black leather couch faced a widescreen TV, again equipped with surround-sound speakers. A hallway off the living area led toward the back of the house and bedrooms, she assumed. Up here, the smell of coffee drowned out that of the carpeting.

In spite of the display of high-quality furniture, the place didn't seem ostentatious. He had good taste too, and a reasonable decorating sense. The lack of a bachelor-pad aura made her wonder if a former girlfriend or an ex-wife had played a part in the decorating, but there was no femininity about it, either. And Julia had said David was currently unattached and had implied he'd been that way for quite some time.

"The guest room is back there." David interrupted her musings, pointing down the hallway. "First door on the right. The bathroom is the next door down. Help yourself if you want to freshen up. I'll see if I can find something for you to wear."

Tony started to tell him that wasn't necessary but stopped her self-sufficiency reflexes just in time. She couldn't spend the rest of the night in this velvet monstrosity. Plus she needed to relax and let him do his thing. It wouldn't kill her to let him be nice to her for a few hours.

She followed David down the short hallway, stopping by the first door while he continued to a doorway at the end of the hall. His bedroom. An image flashed across her mind of him reading in bed, his chest bare. Did he still wear glasses to read? Did he wear pajamas? Or maybe he slept in the buff...

Tony's lips narrowed against her teeth. Frustrated at herself, she yanked open the door to the guest room. She'd had wayward thoughts about men before, but this was getting out of control. Imagining him naked was no way to thank him for giving her the use of his guest room. In fact, it seemed rude. She wondered if Emily Post would have anything to say about the situation.

The guest bedroom had gray carpeting, like the rest of the house, but the curtains and bedspread were rose and maroon, in a geometric pattern. A bit more restful than stark black, Tony thought. And also neat, carefully put together and edging toward masculine. She was almost certain at this point that he was still single.

She laid her purse on the bed. Her wedding invitation poked out through a space behind the clasps. Tony pulled it out, and a pale blue rectangle floated down to land on the floor. David's business card. She picked it up, looked at it, then tucked it back into her purse.

"Here you go."

Tony jumped, startled, then turned to see David leaning in the door, a navy blue sweat suit draped over one arm. He jerked his gaze up to hers, as if he'd been looking somewhere he shouldn't. Was he seriously checking out her ass? Or just trying to figure out if the sweat pants would fit her? She hated to admit how much she liked the idea of the first option.

"I found these for you," he said. "I'm sure they'll be big, but the pants have a drawstring." Tony took the clothes from him, hesitant. Wearing his clothes was certainly unlikely to alleviate her problems. She'd start thinking about what parts of him had touched the clothes before she'd had the privilege of wearing them.

"Thanks," she said.

"All right. I'm going to go change." He closed the door behind him.

And there were those pesky mental pictures again: of David unbuttoning his shirt, peeling his pants down those long legs...

Tony made an annoyed noise at herself and stepped out of her shoes. Then, following another strange impulse, she buried her face in the sweats. Thank God—they smelled like fabric softener. Not a hint of David.

She wiggled out of her nylons and dress and pulled on the sweats. Everything bagged on her, but she was able to cinch the pants tightly enough with the drawstring that there was at least no chance they would fall off.

Belatedly, she realized she had nothing to put on her feet. Maybe David would have a pair of slippers. She didn't want to ask, though. She hated being dependent on anyone, particularly someone of the male persuasion.

From the other room, Tony heard the TV come on, then the rattling of ceramic mugs. David was done, then. Suddenly shy, she adjusted her clothes and eased open the door. Why she was hesitant, she didn't know. The sweat suit was certainly more modest than the dress with its plunging neckline. But it was *his* sweat suit, and his house, and owing him for his hospitality made her uneasy.

The big TV in the living room was tuned to the news, which was about half over. The weatherman gave a tease of the upcoming forecast; then they went to a commercial.

Tony rounded the big sectional couch and sat. The leather was chilly but comforting as the soft cushions took her in. She curled her bare feet under her.

"Want some coffee?" David called from the other room. "It's decaf."

"Sure." She was stuffed from the big dinner, but coffee sounded good. The cold had soaked through her skin and into her bones, and she wanted to dispel it.

"The clothes okay?"

"They're fine. At least they're warm."

David came into the room, a steaming ceramic mug in each hand. Out of his suit and in more casualwear now, he looked just as attractive and somehow more accessible. More touchable. She wondered if the flopping forelock of his brown hair was as soft as it looked. "Are you still cold? I can turn on the fireplace."

Not a good idea. Lighting that lovely fireplace, gas or no, would create a decidedly romantic atmosphere that Tony didn't want to deal with right now. But her tingly cold numb toes told her another story.

"That would be nice."

David flipped a switch and turned a knob to adjust the gas flame. A vent above the fireplace blew hot air into the room. The flow stroked Tony's face.

David settled himself on the couch next to her, too close, as far as Tony was concerned, and passed Tony one of the mugs of coffee. He'd fixed it light, she noticed. She liked it light. She wondered if he'd just guessed, or if he'd been watching her doctor her after-dinner coffee at the wedding. His was light as well, so maybe he'd just made them both the same.

They were quiet for a time, sipping coffee and watching the weather forecast while the room filled up with warmth. Tony hoped for a positive update regarding the weather, but the weatherman didn't show much hope for the storm's being over by morning. The Denver area and the surrounding suburbs had gotten little more than a dusting, but the front had stalled over the mountains and was expected to stay there until some time tomorrow. She wouldn't be going anywhere any time soon, then.

She slid a sidelong glance at David, who was blowing into his coffee mug. He seemed relaxed, comfortable, and the laid-back aura was contagious. She couldn't afford to let her guard down, though, no matter how at home she was beginning to feel. The hominess made her start having thoughts about what it would be like to settle in and have someone to come home to again. Someone who didn't give her the feeling he wanted to be somewhere else.

"Well," Tony said, making a vague gesture toward the TV. "I could be stuck here another day." He'd have to be at least annoyed about that, if she ended up disrupting his routine that long.

He only nodded. "You're welcome to stay as long as you need to." Had he moved closer? Surely not—she would have noticed the actual movement.

She sipped her coffee, juggling her schedule in her head and trying to ignore his gaze resting on her. It made her uncomfortable, nervous about what he might expect to come next. "I'm supposed to start a new job assignment on Monday."

David shrugged. "I'm sure this will have blown over by then."

"But what about my car?"

He leaned forward, resting his elbows on his knees. Again, he seemed closer. He could have easily laid a hand on her knee. She wished he would. No, she didn't. "Don't worry about it. We'll work things out."

We. That was the problem. She really wanted to take care of herself, by herself. This sudden, unavoidable dependence on David made her uncomfortable. Itchy, almost.

"Thank you," she said, because it was the right thing to say, but the words made her feel small and inadequate, like she'd admitted she couldn't take care of herself. David still seemed relaxed, as if he didn't care that Tony had been dumped on him through circumstances beyond her control. Surely she was some kind of inconvenience to him.

She watched him watch the sports report, noticing that he didn't yell at the screen but only made a clucking noise at the current scores. Finally, he leaned back, folding his hands behind his head.

"So," he said, and Tony looked up sharply, responding to the crispness of his tone. He seemed to realize the word had been a bit too abrupt, for his tone was much easier when he finished the thought. "Freak snowstorms aside, did you have a nice time?"

Tony thought she should probably give a pat answer, but instead she heard a more truthful response falling from her mouth. "For the most part. It was a fun evening."

"For the most part?"

Tony shrugged. "It's just... I haven't seen some of those people since graduation. I feel like I'm not even the same person I was then. And some of them...they don't seem to have changed at all."

"I know what you mean." David's sober nod told her he was taking her seriously. He leaned forward, definitely in her personal space now. "I don't feel like the same person, either."

"And Cheryl and Missy... I can't remember why we were best friends." She left it at that, uncertain how to express how she'd felt in the face of her former friends' vacuousness. Not without sounding like a hypocrite, at any rate. Who was she to judge anyone else's life choices? Hers hadn't been exactly stellar.

David shrugged. "You were in the same social circles. You hang with people who do the same things you do. It's human nature."

"You sound like you've given this way too much thought." Tony cringed when she heard what she'd said. It seemed thoughtless, casually offensive without intending to be. Or was she overreacting again? She'd spent so long under the constant scrutiny of Rudy's judgment that she still second-guessed everything she said and did.

But David laughed. "I probably have. I spend way too much time in my own head. Occupational hazard." He was quiet a moment, studying her. The weight of his gaze made her self-conscious in a way she hadn't felt in a long time. As if he liked what he saw. As if he valued her.

Had Rudy ever looked at her like that? He had, she remembered. When he'd come to pick her up for their senior prom. He'd had that open look of love that had made Tony feel like she could do anything. Like they could do anything. At their wedding, small as it had been, his attention had been all for her, but even then it had already been tinged with something. Something that had grown and grown and eventually broken them.

It was hard to look at David's eyes, so full of promise, and not think about that little seed that had grown so inexorably and fatally between her and Rudy.

"I'm glad you enjoyed yourself," he went on. "After I found out you and Rudy split, I thought maybe seeing everybody from high school might have made you uncomfortable." He ended the statement with a questioning look, as if he expected her to elaborate, maybe spill her entire sordid story.

That was really, really not going to happen. "Maybe a little. But I enjoyed seeing Julia, and dancing…" *Dancing with you.* Another little nugget she wasn't going to admit to.

He smiled, though. Obviously he was perfectly capable of finishing that sentence all on his own. "I enjoyed the dancing, too." He shifted his hand then, and his fingers brushed her thigh, just behind her knee. Just subtle enough to seem like an accident, just well aimed enough that she knew it wasn't.

The tingle of happiness she'd started to sense suddenly disappeared. "I'm tired," she said, searching for any excuse to get away from the hint of promise in David's eyes. "Would you mind if I went ahead and crashed?"

He hesitated, and for a weird moment she thought he was going to tell her no, she wasn't allowed to go to sleep yet. Instead, he said, "Are you okay?"

"I'm fine. I just..." How did she explain? *You want something from me and I can't figure out what it is and I'm not ready to give anybody anything yet so back the hell off.* No, that wouldn't do it. But he was so close and so warm, and everything about him drew her to him. "I'm just really tired. It's been a long day."

He nodded, his eyes too shrewd, as if they knew too much. She could tell he didn't quite believe her, knew she was hiding something. "Okay." He pushed his feet. "Let me show you the guest bathroom. We'll see if we can scare you up some toothpaste."

The bed was cozy, with clean-smelling sheets and a heavy comforter. Tony crawled in and flipped off the light.

The absolute darkness startled her. After so long living in town, she'd forgotten the deep, dark of night in the mountains. With snow and stars obscured by snow clouds, the only light in the room came from the hall light seeping faintly in under the door. She buried herself to her neck in the blankets and stared into the darkness.

This was not how she'd planned to spend her weekend. Of course, it wasn't what David had planned, either. She really just wanted to go home, to her own bed, get herself mentally ready for her new temp assignment, eat chocolate, watch some shows off her DVR, go shopping, maybe buy some new shoes. None of that was going to happen. Instead, apparently, she was going to lie here in David's guest bedroom and brood.

She couldn't figure out why she felt so strange. Just being in David's presence seemed to drag up all the yuck she'd tried to shove under the carpet when she finally ended her marriage. Why was it rolling up its ugly underbelly again when she found herself with someone who was acting like he might be interested in her?

And what was all this nonsense about him being infatuated with her in high school? She'd never been aware of any particular interest on his part, much less a crush or infatuation. Surely she would've noticed.

Then again, she hadn't paid much attention to him. She'd used him once to help her get through an algebra exam. She couldn't characterize the interaction any more charitably; she'd been nice to him while he been tutoring her, then, when the exams were over, had snubbed him. A minor sin, maybe, but it gave her a twinge of guilt when she thought about it now. Especially when he was being nice to her.

A half hour of brooding broodiness later, Tony looked at the clock and discovered only five minutes had passed. With an exasperated sigh, she sat up and turned on the light. After a moment's thought, she slipped out of bed and opened the bedroom door.

A soft murmur of music drifted down the hallway. David's bedroom door was partly open, and a light burned beyond it. Tony padded to the door and peered around it.

Yet another computer occupied a desk in a corner of the bedroom. David sat in front of it, his back to the door. Hesitantly, she knocked.

He turned to face her. He wore glasses now, lightweight wire frames with thin lenses. They made him look bookish but not at all unattractive. Tony became suddenly, acutely aware of where she was and tried very hard not to look at the bed.

"What's wrong?" he asked.

"Nothing really." His quilt was maroon and black, she noticed, a geometric pattern that complemented the one in the guest room. "I just can't sleep."

David grinned and reached over to pull some paper out of the printer tray. His sweatshirt rode up when he bent over, and Tony had a hard time convincing herself she shouldn't look at his bare skin. The shirt settled back into place as he straightened.

"Here you go," he said, handing her the paper and a pen.

Tony shook her head, not willing to admit he'd given her exactly what she needed. But she'd always sketched when she was nervous, even in high school. He'd kidded her about it more than once.

She should just leave now, she thought, but before she could stop herself, she said, "Do you, um...wear contacts now, or did you have Lasik?"

He smiled. "Lasik. I only wear glasses now at night, when my eyes are tired, or when I've been on the computer a long time. It was totally worth it."

"I'll bet. So what are you working on? Another game?"

He rolled his chair to one side so she could see the screen. Crudely rendered stick figures stood posed in battle in front of a background of color blocks.

"*Dark Princes III*," he said. "It's a really early version. We still don't have the artwork hashed out, so we're just blocking out some of the major action sequences. Rich and I wrote up the plot along with one of our other programmers. The other programmer wasn't happy about the predominately male characters in the first two games, so we took her advice, and now *Dark Princes III* is about Prince Aelfwyn's sister Aethelfried."

"Well, that's a nice change of pace, anyway. Those adventure games always seem so sexist." Belatedly, Tony noticed her clipped tone.

David only grinned. "Touché. Actually, I'd always intended to move into some more gender-flexible games, but the *Dark Princes* plot didn't lend itself too well to that, and games with male leads are proven to sell better."

"Why is that?" asked Tony.

"Supposedly women don't have a problem playing games where they're presenting themselves as a male character, but men aren't so happy pretending they're a female character. A few games have bucked the standard, but with *Dark Princes* being a new franchise, I decided to play it safe."

"I see." Tony paused, evaluating her tone. Had she sounded too snippy? "I guess video games are a man's world too." Just like everything else. Yeah, that had sounded a little snippy. She needed to work on that.

David didn't seem offended. He turned back toward the computer and touched a button. The stick figures came to life, moving into confrontation. "The world is what you make of it."

Maybe for you. Tony managed to quash that thought before she voiced it aloud. Some people turned everything they touched to gold. Others turned it to mud.

She started to back out of the room, then paused, watching the little stick figures bash each other with stick-figure swords. Their movements were jerky, unrefined, but even at this stage, she could tell the choreography of the battle had been carefully thought out. They just needed clothes. And skin and muscles and, well, faces would be good too. Pictures started to form in her mind of what they might look like, pictures that made the tips of her fingers long to hold a pencil, to work it all out where she could see it.

"What got you interested in this line of work?" she heard herself asking.

He glanced back over his shoulder. "I spent a lot of time in front of video game consoles in high school and college. It seemed like a natural progression."

"I guess you always were good at math." *Lame, Tony.* She really didn't know what developing computer games involved, though, other than the obvious programming skills.

He chuckled. Even her lamest lameness didn't seem to faze him much. "I am that. And I can barf up C++ code with both hands tied behind my back, typing with my nose."

It was an interesting image on numerous levels. "I'd like to see that."

"I bet you would." He swiveled his chair so that he faced her more directly. Her eyes caught on the line of his throat, the curve of it as it disappeared behind his collar. His heartbeat pulsed in the groove along the side of his neck, and there was a small spot just under his chin where he hadn't shaved quite cleanly. "Anyway, I studied computer science in college, where I met Rich, and we decided to take the jump and start marketing our own games."

"Rich programs too?"

"Yeah, and he has a better eye for art than I do, so he recruited our initial graphic artists. Now we have a department for that, and he runs it. Good artists are hard to find." His gaze seemed to narrow on her little, as if he were trying to tell her something. She didn't know what that might be. She certainly didn't know anything about art for computer games. Sure, she knew her way around Photoshop, but she was going to be an accountant, so it wasn't really relevant knowledge. Uncomfortable under his attention, she lifted the hand that held the paper.

"Thanks for the paper."

"Any time." His smile was warm. She wanted to get away—wanted to move closer. She could almost feel his touch again, the casual, not-quite-accidental tracery of his fingers against her thigh. God, she really needed to get out of here. His gaze weighed heavy on her as she turned and headed back to the guest room.

The bed had grown chilly in her absence, and it took a few minutes for Tony's body heat to soak the sheets again. With the pile of paper propped in her lap—not exactly steady but steady enough for her use—she began to sketch.

She started doodling; then that mysterious something took over, and she found the lines shaping a horse, a woman on its back, dressed in war gear. She slid out of the warm bed to kneel next to the nightstand, spreading papers out under the light of the lamp. With the wider, harder surface, the picture became more intricate until she had produced something that looked more like a professionally finished product than a doodle.

She moved to another sheet and started another—a dragon in flight against a backdrop of snowcapped mountains. Discussing David's game must have triggered something in her subconscious. She hadn't drawn a dragon in years.

Tony finished that picture and moved to another. She could lose everything in the act of drawing: tension, insecurity, insomnia. She felt alive when she drew, as if her soul found its true purpose in the point where pen met paper.

Every time she drew, she wondered why she kept pushing this need away. It made her feel so...herself. The doubts and insecurities, the fluttery tension that made her day-to-day living so twitchy at times, disappeared when she let herself draw.

The pen moved across the paper in a flat arc, then moved downward. Along the same theme as the wedding, as the dragon, she drew a man in armor, a big, two-handed sword balanced between his hands, its tip resting on the ground. It wasn't until she had sketched in the eyes and started to outline the long, strong nose that she realized she was drawing someone who looked very much like David.

Chapter Three

Though he'd been up until nearly three a.m., David found himself wide awake at eight. He'd spent a good portion of the night staring up at the ceiling, wondering if Tony was okay, if she was warm enough, if she needed an extra blanked or another pillow, if she'd left the sweats on or if she'd taken them off to sleep naked... In short, thoughts not conducive to a good night's sleep. Not that it mattered. He could catch a nap later this afternoon, if he chose. Best just to accept it and have a cup of coffee.

He knocked gently on Tony's door, in case she was awake and hesitant to roam the house while he slept. No answer. David paused. He knew it wasn't exactly the best etiquette regarding an overnight guest, but he wanted to be sure she was all right. Carefully, silently, he opened the door.

She lay on her back, head tilted to one side, her dark blonde hair spread about her on the pillows. He'd always thought she was easily the prettiest girl in school. Her hair had been golden-blonde then—now it was the color of raw honey. Gold lashes lay against her cheeks. She had the blankets wrapped up around her shoulders, her face half covered and her knees drawn up. He wondered if she was cold.

She was so beautiful. He'd never met another woman who stirred him the way she did. And it was more than just lust or the remnants of a high school crush.

Or was it? He eased the door shut and went to the kitchen to start his coffee. He'd felt like a teenager again when she'd danced with him. She'd been so soft and sweet, cradled against his chest. And, just like a teenager, he'd had to deal with hormonal surges that made his body do things he hoped she wouldn't notice. Not much he could do about that, though. And he didn't feel too guilty about it, given the feelings that had provoked it. Not just lust, that was certain. So much more. At least he knew his libido was still healthy. He'd ignored it for so long to focus on business concerns, he'd been beginning to wonder if it might atrophy.

He'd asked her to dance one other time, at their Junior prom, and she'd turned him down in no uncertain terms. He'd spent several weeks before prom helping her study for her algebra finals and had hoped she might be willing to give him one dance since they'd spent so much time together. But she'd administered a direct snub and proceeded to dance with Rudy.

He'd thought of joking with her about that night, since she'd finally agreed to dance with him after all these years, but had decided against it. If she'd taken it wrong, he might have missed the chance to enjoy her company. And he didn't know how to make the joke light enough to keep her from reacting badly. Besides, he doubted she even remembered the earlier incident. And she'd felt so good, so right in his arms, that he hadn't wanted to break the spell.

The coffee bubbled and hissed, filling the kitchen with its rich, dark aroma. The smell evoked endless mornings at home, when his father would wake up before the sun to begin his morning commute to Vail, where he'd managed a hotel. David's mother would be awake, bleary-eyed in a red terrycloth robe, making oatmeal while the coffee perked.

David wondered what memories Tony had of her childhood mornings. Not of Mom and Dad, that was certain. Her parents had divorced when Tony was six. Her mother had struggled to raise her two daughters. Her mornings with a single mother had undoubtedly been hectic, probably difficult. And her mother had always seemed stressed to him. Worried. In high school, Tony had seemed mostly unaffected by this, but now David wondered. Had uncertainty and stress at home affected her more than her favored status in school? It seemed likely.

Pouring his coffee and doctoring it with cream and sugar, he reflected that he knew a great deal about Tony, yet really nothing at all. High school history didn't count anymore. The news of her divorce had surprised him, as had her decision to abandon her dreams of a career as an artist. On the outside, she'd changed not at all, but on deeper levels, she was a different person. A person who could still make him lose half his sense with a look.

Soft noises drifted from the hallway, and David turned to see Tony padding on bare feet toward the kitchen. Her hair was prettily mussed, her eyes puffy. David smiled. The sight of her made him feel not just protective but possessive. He wanted to claim her. He hoped it didn't show on his face. It was too much, really. Not for him, but for her. The strength of his emotions would probably scare her off, but he felt strangely ready to grapple with them. Maybe because they weren't new to him. And if there was one thing he knew how to do, it was how to change something he wanted into something he had.

"Good morning," he said.

Tony pushed her hair back from her face. "Hi."

She came to the counter to stand next to him, leaning toward the coffeemaker. Closing her eyes, she breathed the aroma and the steam. David went to the cabinet to retrieve a cup. She took it from him, fingers barely brushing his, and smiled. Her normally green eyes were almost gray. He wondered if they always looked like that in the morning. A small part of his mind wondered what it would be like to wake up like this with her every day. A larger part of his mind decided he was going to find out.

"Thanks." Her voice was a bit gravelly. "It smells wonderful."

"Did you sleep okay?"

"Once I got to sleep, yes. Thanks for the paper. Drawing always helps. I don't know why."

"You're welcome." He sipped his coffee, wondering if he should venture into less neutral territory. "It's you. It's what you do."

She nodded almost absently. He couldn't tell if she wasn't really paying attention or if she was dismissing the comment. Either way, he pushed on. "So why don't you do it anymore?"

Her gaze flicked toward him, then back to her coffee. "I'm on my own. I need to be practical to be sure the bills get paid."

He didn't know how to respond to that. He'd followed his dreams and had found his way to success, and it was hard for him to see her choosing a path he thought would ultimately make her unhappy. Then again, she had a point.

"I was sorry to hear about your divorce," he finally said. "What happened?" Bad question. He hurried to fix the gaffe. "I shouldn't have asked that."

She shrugged. "I was young. I did a stupid thing. Now it's over." She sipped her coffee without looking at him. "How's the weather?"

David glanced out the window. She could have seen for herself it was still snowing. Her jaw had gone taut, and he knew she was clamping her emotions down again. Best to let it all lie. "I don't think we'll be going anywhere for a while, but I think it's slowing down."

"Maybe a tow truck could get through?"

"Maybe."

He was disappointed she was so eager to leave. To the high school geek her presence had partially unearthed in him, it felt like another brush-off. On a practical level, though, he understood. It was no fun being stranded away from your own house and clothes. He would have been happy to let her stay here a week, a month—the rest of her life—but of course she couldn't. He had to let her go, so in the meantime, he had to make these moments count.

"Why don't you go ahead and call the auto club?" he suggested. "The phone's over there."

"Probably a good idea."

She went back to the guest room and returned with her auto club card. While she dialed, David rummaged in the cupboard for breakfast cereal. He had finished his first bowl when Tony hung the phone up and joined him at the table, a long look on her face.

"They won't be able to make it out until early this evening, and then only if the snow lets up." She put her face in her hands, rubbing her eyes. "I really have to get to this job in the morning. It's a new assignment from the temp agency. Even if there are extenuating circumstances, you just can't miss the first day. It looks bad."

David poured another bowl of cereal. "You do what you have to do, I guess, but I hope it won't come to that. Cereal?"

Dealing with David

"Thank you." She took the box. "You've really been very kind, David. I don't deserve this kind of treatment, especially from you."

"What do you mean?"

"You know what I mean." Again, her gaze slid away from his. "I was awful to you. Is it too late to apologize for prom?"

He gave her a wry smile. "I don't think so."

"And I could have talked to the football team, told them to quit being douchebags to you. They might not have listened, but...I should have done something. I feel bad that I didn't."

He shrugged. She was taking too much responsibility onto herself, but it had been a bad time for him, and he couldn't quite think of a way to make light of it. "That was a long time ago," he finally said.

She looked at him then, her eyes sad. He'd seen her sad far too often. "That doesn't make it right."

"Well, I didn't notice anyone trying to pants me or sit me on the fountain last night." He paused, then swept a hand dramatically toward his semi-opulent surroundings. "And now I have my revenge."

Tony smiled, which was exactly what he'd wanted. She also flushed, which surprised him. "That's true." She leaned back in her chair, stirring her cereal. "Yes, revenge is definitely yours."

He chuckled, happy that she seemed happy for him, happy she was here. "Eat your breakfast. Did you talk to Mike at all last night? You remember him, don't you? I think he was a tight end or something. He owns a repair shop near here. I'll give him a call in a couple of hours and see if there's anything he can do to help with your car."

"Thanks. I appreciate that."

They chatted a bit more, but David hardly paid attention. He was too busy watching the way her eyes changed color in the shifting morning light, and the graceful curve of her hand on her spoon. Finishing off the last of his increasingly soggy cereal, he made a vow to himself.

He wasn't letting her get away this time.

As it turned out, Mike was able to do quite a lot. A manic collector of auto parts, he actually had what was needed to fix Tony's car. He had it running by midafternoon, then, much to Tony's surprise, gave her a fifty-percent discount.

"This really isn't necessary," she said, handing him her credit card.

His first attempt at a reply was drowned out by a passing snowplow. The snow had finally let up just before noon, and the plows had been busy since. Mike tried again.

"If I can't give discounts to old friends, then who can I give discounts to?" He charged the reduced rate to her card and handed it back to her.

"Well, thank you," Tony said.

She appreciated the gesture, although sometimes it seemed everyone was trying too hard to take care of her. After all, Mike was hardly an old friend. She'd known him only superficially in high school, and then only because he'd been on the football team and had hung out with Rudy.

Come to think of it, she'd known everyone in high school only superficially. Even Rudy, as it had turned out. And especially David. She'd thought she had him filed into the right place in her head—the overly studious, boring, socially awkward geek who could help you with your homework but would kill your popularity with extended exposure. And now he was standing next to her in the cramped quarters of the small repair shop, watching her, watching out for her, and nothing about him fit any categories she could conjure. He was no longer classifiable. It made her nervous. And warm. And made it hard to remember what last name she was using these days when she went to sign her charge slip.

She handed the charge slip to Mike, hoping he wouldn't notice the little scribble where she'd started to write "Antonytte James," then turned to David. He was about three-quarters of an inch too close, and she blinked, resisting the urge to take an obvious step backward.

"I'll give you a call next week so I can return your clothes." She'd intended to change back into her dress, huge and cumbersome as it was, but David had insisted she wear his sweats instead. "When are you most likely to be available?"

"I'm planning to be in the Lakewood office on Friday. Give me a call Friday morning, and we'll do lunch."

"All right, but only on one condition."

His mouth quirked into a half smile. "What's that?"

"It's on me."

The smile turned to a grin. "You drive a hard bargain, but I accept."

Tony couldn't help smiling back. "All right. I'll talk to you Friday." Then she didn't know whether she should hug him, shake his hand or just run away while she had the chance. It didn't help that Mike seemed far too interested in their discussion.

Finally, she stuck out her hand and shook David's firmly. God, his hand was big.

"Friday," she said. "I'll call you." Then, with that inanity echoing behind her, she escaped to her newly repaired car.

Snowplows had cleared the highway, but some snowpack remained, in spite of the heavy coating of sand that had followed the plowing, making driving a bit slippery. Tony gripped the wheel and prayed a blessing on her antilock brakes. She'd kicked off her pumps—unfortunately David hadn't had any shoes to fit her—and her feet, in borrowed socks, felt funny on the pedals. It would be a long drive home.

The snow, though, broke up about halfway down the mountain. Where there had been nearly three feet at Eagle Creek, where the elevation was close to ten thousand feet, there was only six inches or so once she reached the foothills, and the accumulation steadily decreased as she descended toward the suburbs. With less concentration needed for driving, she found her mind drifting.

It had seemed unlikely at the time, but she'd actually enjoyed the hours she'd spent with David. He had filled her morning by demonstrating his prototype of *Dark Princes III*, as well as *Dark Princes II*, which wouldn't be in stores for two more weeks. Tony had become quite absorbed in the games, but perhaps more absorbed in his warmth and smell as he leaned in behind her to point at the screen, or in the touch of his hand against hers as he helped her guide the mouse. His breath had caressed her ear, along with his voice.

You've just been without a man for too long. As bitter as her breakup with Rudy had been, she sometimes missed his warm bulk in bed next to her. After all, their marriage hadn't been all bad. They'd been happy for a while.

Yeah, when we were both too stupid to know better. Well, now she was smarter. Jaded and world-wise and not about to jump into anything, particularly another relationship.

And why was she thinking of David in those terms, anyway? He'd done her a great favor, but that was all. She'd buy him lunch, return his clothes and that would be it.

Right. Because telling herself that over and over would make the butterflies in her stomach go away. Or stop the warm fuzzies she got whenever she thought about him. She didn't like the fact that he did these way too pleasant things to her psyche. It was a bad sign.

Besides, if he was so awesome, why wasn't he attached? He had good looks, money, a nice house, a cool car—there had to be something wrong with him. Maybe he was relationship-shy too, or secretly a control freak like Rudy had been. He owned his own business, after all. She should just get the hell out before she actually got in.

Then again, maybe she should interrogate Julia. Julia knew things. Julia could provide Important Information.

Annoyed with herself, she flipped on the radio and cranked it up to drown out her scurrying mind. If Nirvana turned up full blast couldn't remind her that life pretty much sucked, she didn't know what could.

It was nearing dinnertime when she pulled into the parking lot of her apartment complex. Home had never looked so good. There was only a dusting of snow on the parking lot, so she pulled off the baggy socks and slipped back into her pumps.

There were two messages on her voice mail, both from Julia. The second one sounded worried, so Tony called her right away.

After three rings, Julia's voice mail kicked in. They were probably out recovering from being snowed in.

"I'm fine," Tony told the phone. "Just got home. Got caught in the storm, and my car died. Call me when you get a chance. Glad to hear the baby's feeling better."

She microwaved some leftovers for dinner, then tried to watch TV, but nothing caught her attention. Finally, following an inexplicable urge, she dug through the back of her bedroom closet until she found her high school yearbooks.

And there they all were. Tony looking fresh and young, her hair longer and lighter from spending so much time in the sun. Rudy, thick-necked and handsome, wearing number twelve on his football jersey, a shock of black hair partially obscuring his blue eyes. And David, scarecrow-thin, eyes like fishbowls, but now she could see the seed of the man he had become. She could see that in Rudy, as well, in the curl of his lip, the glint of arrogance in his eyes. If she'd only known then...

She closed the book and closed her eyes, and in a few minutes, she had drifted into a dream. Rudy was there, a big, black-clad knight like the knights in *Dark Princes*, and David rode up on a palomino stallion and chopped off Rudy's head.

Chapter Four

By Wednesday morning, the two feet of snow at Eagle Creek had settled, melted and sublimated to something less than twelve inches. David stood drinking coffee on his deck, looking out over the white yard. Tracks of at least a half dozen elk crisscrossed the snow. A black, tufted-eared Abert's squirrel berated him from a nearby pine tree, while a crow cawed raucously somewhere above his head. In the distance, the massive peaks of the Continental Divide hulked white into a brilliantly cloudless sky.

All of it served to remind him why he had returned here after so long on the East Coast. There weren't so many people here, not as much rush and bustle, and even when he was working on a tight deadline, he could enjoy the illusion of quiet and peace.

He was having trouble concentrating, though, these last few days. He'd planned to work out of his house for most of the week, finishing up the *Dark Princes III* prototype, then spending Friday at the Lakewood office taking care of busywork and going over things with Rich. But that meant waiting until Friday to see Tony again, and right now that struck him as a bad plan.

He'd been back and forth with himself ever since he'd watched Tony drive off in the remnants of Saturday's snowstorm. He wanted to see her again, but part of him thought it wasn't such a good idea. It was the same part that had had those nasty, ulterior motives for going to the wedding. The same part that had wanted to drive the Mercedes, just to see his classmates drool.

As it turned out, he wasn't the only graduate of Eagle Creek High School who could afford a Mercedes. He was, however, probably the only one who could afford a Lamborghini. The thought made him laugh at himself for being so petty. The money had been much better spent on raises, additional hires and new equipment.

Yes, the desire to rub his former classmates' noses in his success had definitely been a motive for attending the wedding. Until he'd seen Tony, and all the old feelings had come rushing back at him, except stronger in their way. More mature. Harder to ignore. Having her in his house hadn't helped. He already missed her. He'd actually entertained the thought, for a moment, that spending time with her might help him forget that long-ago crush. It hadn't worked. Instead, it had started his brain plotting an entirely different course.

He finished his coffee and headed back into the house. He had work to do and no inclination to do it. There was too much nonsense rattling around in his head.

There was no point running from his feelings for Tony if they weren't real, nor was there any point pursuing them. The question was, how to determine if they were real? The only answer he could frame was to see her again, maybe a few times, to see if he was truly attracted to her or just reliving adolescent fantasies. How many times? Many times, his brain answered. Then he wondered if he should make a spreadsheet. Track each date, how long it lasted, if attraction increased or decreased afterward. There could be pivot tables. Maybe pie charts.

Wow, that was a terrible plan. But just the fact he'd thought about it made him realize how important this quest was becoming to him.

"I'm really way too old for this," he told nobody. He fetched his cell phone from the charger and poked around until he found Julia's number in his contacts list.

As luck would have it, Julia had spoken to Tony Monday night and had Tony's new work number. Ten a.m. was late enough to call, he figured, and dialed her number.

He was transferred a couple of times before he finally heard, "Hello? This is Antonytte Mullin."

"Hey, Tony. It's David."

A moment of silence betrayed her surprise, but her voice was calm. "Hi. I wasn't expecting to talk to you until Friday."

"I hope you don't mind my calling. I got your number from Julia."

"No, it's fine. Just a surprise, that's all."

"Good. Look, I've had a change of plans, and I'm going to be down in Lakewood today as well as Friday. I was wondering if you might be free for lunch?"

"Actually, it looks like I'm going to be free the whole afternoon." There were bitter tones in her voice, and David was tempted to ask about it, but Tony went on. "Sure. I could use a diversion today. Can you meet me at Old Chicago on South Wadsworth at one?"

David found himself grinning, pleased at her take-charge attitude. "Sure. I'll see you there."

As he ended the call, his stomach flip-flopped. He wanted to see her again. Too much, he thought. He wanted to be able to take this carefully, logically, and he couldn't if his emotions kept roller coastering on him. He had a lot on his plate these days. A lot in his life. As much as he wanted to explore what might develop between himself and Tony, he couldn't help but think he was setting himself up to be cold-shouldered again at the metaphorical prom.

Old Chicago, home of 110 beers and deep-dish pizza, wasn't terribly crowded at one on a Wednesday afternoon. David parked his Jeep in a spot near the door, looking for Tony's Honda.

He didn't see it, so he put down a window and settled himself to wait. No point going inside on such a nice day. In typical Colorado fashion, the weather had turned warm and breezy a few days after the snowstorm, and today the thermometer nudged seventy.

Tony pulled up about five minutes later. She seemed harried, her movements quick and jerky as she got out of the car. She was wearing a business casual pantsuit in a dark jade green, and her hair was drawn back in a matching clip. She didn't even look to see if he was there—just stomped toward the front door, looking at the ground, brow deeply furrowed. David clambered out of his car and jogged to catch up with her.

"Hey," he called.

She slowed down and looked at him, her face softening. "Hey." Her eyes slid down to his chest, taking in the bright tie he wore with a lightweight dress shirt. "Pinky and the Brain," she said. "You have good taste in cartoons." She smiled, but turmoil still lurked in her eyes.

"What's wrong?" He hopped to get ahead of her and opened the door.

"I hate my job."

"How can you hate it? You just started."

"They promised me full time, and now they're telling me they only need me half days. And I thought I was going to be doing data entry, and instead I'm filing and fetching coffee..." She waved of her hand. "I don't want to talk about it. Just give me a chance to cool down."

The restaurant didn't provide an intimate atmosphere, but the hostess seated them at a corner table, and the place was fairly quiet. David pulled Tony's chair out for her. She smiled, and some of the worry lines in her face relaxed.

"Thank you, David," she said, sounding genuinely grateful.

He sat across from her. "I was afraid you might be offended by such chauvinistic gestures." He meant it as a joke, and it seemed to work, as she chuckled quietly.

"There's a difference between chauvinism and chivalry."

"My mother always says it's just plain manners." He picked up the menu but didn't open it. "Besides, I wanted to see you smile."

She looked away and down, a flush rising on her face. "I'm sorry. I'm just really frustrated. In fact, I have been for a long time. Temping pays the rent—barely—but everywhere I go I'm 'the temp'. And apparently it's socially acceptable to screw the temp over whenever necessary."

"So you don't get no respect?"

Tony smiled again. "Not one blessed bit."

A waitress arrived, and they placed an order. David folded his hands on the table. "You don't get any...support or anything from Rudy?"

Her eyes flashed, and he knew he'd stepped over the line. *Not your business. Why are you an idiot, David?*

"When I threw him out, I threw him *out*," she said emphatically. "I don't want anything from that man, especially not his money."

"I'm sorry. I shouldn't have said anything."

She eased up, settling back in her chair. "No, I'm sorry. I didn't realize I was still so touchy about it." Blowing out a breath, she pushed back a few stray strands of hair and focused on her menu. Her cheeks had colored.

He wanted to know more but knew he couldn't ask. It was none of his business. But he couldn't help wondering about her. Worrying about her. What wounds lay behind her neatly turned-out exterior, with her well-tailored suit and her neatly confined hair? More importantly, how could he salve those wounds? Being this close to her wasn't helping him sort out his feelings. It just brought them crashing down on him again. He wanted to reach across the table and hold her hand, slip a finger beneath a stray lock of hair and thread it behind her ear. It felt different, though, from what he'd felt for her as a teenager—quieter, deeper, less desperate. He wanted to take her off to his cave—not to hide her away but to protect her. More Cro-Magnon than Neanderthal, cave-wise.

"So," she said. "You never got married?"

He shook his head. "No. I haven't even dated much. In college I was too busy; then I was focused on getting the business started and convinced myself I didn't have time for anything else." Never mind that he had always been awkward and stupid around women. Never mind that the last woman he'd dated had only been interested in his money. And never mind that in the back of his mind had always lingered an image of Tony.

"Was it worth it? Putting your personal life on hold, I mean."

"I guess I don't know yet. It's better than rushing into something, though."

Too late, he realized what he'd said. Tony's mouth tightened as if she held back a retort.

"I'm sorry," David said hastily. "That's not what I meant... I mean, I didn't mean you..." He stammered and wasn't even sure what he was saying. He could feel his cheeks getting hot, and suddenly his hands felt twice as big as normal. It was like he'd been struck by a transfiguration spell that had turned him into his sixteen-year-old, hopelessly geeky, socially inept self. It wasn't a good feeling.

Tony's face gentled. He had the feeling she was trying not to laugh at him.

"It's okay," she said. "I made some mistakes." Her eyes met his with a warmth in them he'd never hoped to see. "A lot of mistakes," she added, and her gaze moved away from his.

Desire moved hot through David's blood. He wanted to take her in his arms and kiss her until she forgot about everything that had ever hurt her in the past. Then he wanted to just kiss her senseless, and that was only for starters. The strength of it almost frightened him. He had to back off, and fast, take more time to analyze his feelings before something irrevocable happened. Pivot tables, he thought. Pie charts.

"Anyway," Tony went on, "I learned my lesson. From now on, it's slow and thoughtful, no more rash and stupid."

David nodded with a rueful smile. Her message was clear enough.

"Probably the best approach," he said, "although sometimes if you move too slowly, you miss a good thing."

"I guess I'll have to take that chance."

If he hadn't known better, he would have said her look was coy. But surely she wasn't flirting with him.

David poked at the ice cubes in his Coke with his straw, afraid to respond to what he thought he'd seen. Either he'd offend her by pushing, or he'd revert to teenagerness and make a complete idiot out of himself. He had a feeling the latter was more likely.

After a moment he looked back at her. The quirky expression, if it had been there at all, was gone. He changed the subject.

"So tell me your best temp stories."

The conversation remained in neutral territory until they had finished. David let Tony pay for the meal, as promised, then followed her out to her car, where she had stowed his borrowed clothes in the trunk. She opened it and removed a paper grocery bag, holding it out to him.

"Here are your things. Thanks again for everything."

He took the bag. His fingers touched hers, which were slim and warm, and then they slid away. Her soft expression tugged at him. Her lips were slightly parted, her eyes betraying an uncharacteristic vulnerability. David cleared his throat.

"Listen, if you're having trouble finding work you like, call the Human Resources people at my office. I'm sure we could find you something more interesting than filing."

Her eyes changed suddenly, as if she'd pulled the shades down to close him out. Her mouth thinned, her stance shifting as if she were on guard against a physical blow. Her voice, though, was calm and neutral.

"I'll think about it. Thanks for the offer."

David took a step backward, not certain what he'd done wrong but sure it was time to ease off. There was one thing he had to ask, though. One risk he had to take. "Are you free Friday night? I know I said Friday for lunch before, but..."

Her eyes widened. "Um... I'm not sure."

"If you are, would you like to have dinner?"

"I...I don't know." She reached behind her, fingers closing on the handle of the driver's side door of her car. "Um... How soon would you have to know?"

"Call me Friday at work. Any time before seven."

"All right. I'll let you know."

"Great. Talk to you then."

It took a great effort not to look back as he walked to his car. After he started the ignition, he finally glanced her way. She was already gone.

David realized he wasn't maintaining the proper distance from his situation when, at the end of the day, he was disappointed he hadn't heard from Tony.

"These are all my calls?" he asked his secretary for the third time, sorting through the stack of pink memo slips. He pulled his cell phone out again, as well, to see if any voice mails had registered since he'd last looked at it about three minutes ago. There weren't any voice mails on his office phone, either. Or emails, or text messages, or any other sign she'd tried to contact him.

He'd spent most of the afternoon with Rich, playing the *Dark Princes III* prototype. Which was more taxing than it sounded, because they'd found a half-dozen glitches and at least two logic lapses in the plotline.

"That's all, Mr. Peterson," said the secretary. He'd told her about nine times to call him David, but she was young and insecure and apparently didn't think it was appropriate. She tapped her pencil on the desk. "Um...were you expecting a call?"

David shook his head. "No, not really. Thanks, Nancy."

He thought about Tony all the way home. Images from today mixed with memories. Had they both grown past the ideas that had kept them apart? Or was he just losing himself in something that never had been and never could be?

He stopped at the stop sign just outside Eagle Creek. To go home, he should turn left. Instead, he drove straight ahead.

The Peterson Family Mansion, as David's mother called it, sat on five mountainous acres just north of Eagle Creek proper. In spite of the acreage, there wasn't much in the way of usable property; it was mostly slopes and rocks. But as a kid, David had hiked up the hill and found a narrow stream running through it, and a tree where his oldest brother, fifteen years his senior, had carved his initials accompanied by those of a mysterious "L.M." David had no idea who the girl had been—all he knew was that his sister-in-law had never been an "L.M."

David looked up the slope into the trees as he got out of the car, half tempted to head up to the little stream. There was too much snow to wade through, though, and he'd probably find little more than a vague dent in a snowbank to mark the water's location. Instead, he mounted the stairs to the front door and knocked.

"David!" His mother, a good foot shorter than he, with black hair streaked with striking gray, squeezed him happily around the chest. "I didn't know you were coming by."

He stepped past her into the cozy living room. "I hadn't planned on it. Sort of a last-minute thing."

"Well, I'm glad you did. Sit down, hon. I'm on the phone with your brother. I'll be right there."

David sat on the couch. It was the same old, squashy thing they'd had since David was ten, though he'd finally convinced them to replace the garish burnt orange upholstery with more neutral brown and beige. He couldn't blame them for wanting to keep it. It was stuffed with memories, and comfortable too. He leaned back in the deep cushions and dropped his feet on the coffee table.

"Take your shoes off if you're going to put your feet on the table," Maddy called from the kitchen.

David grinned. He had no idea how she did it. He was completely out of her line of sight, and he doubted she could hear his heels touch the wood from the other room. But she always knew.

"Yes, Mom," he said and obligingly removed his shoes.

Maddy rounded the corner from the kitchen, carrying a cordless phone. From the conversation, David gathered she was talking to his brother, Chris, the younger of David's two older siblings. Chris was twelve years older than David and lived in Seattle.

These days, people would have referred to David as a change-of-life baby, but twenty-seven years ago, they referred to such births as accidents. Lovingly, in the case of David's parents. He had grown up basically an only child, since his brothers were so much older, and so felt somewhat responsible for them. Plus he had the money to take care of them, and the freedom to live wherever he chose, so he'd moved back to Eagle Creek.

"All right, Chris," Maddy was saying. "You take care of yourself. Tell Sherry I said hi. David's here, so I have to go. Okay. Bye."

She hung up the phone. "Do you want anything to drink, David?"

"No, thanks, Mom."

She came to sit next to him on the couch. "It's good to see you. Your father should be home in an hour or so. You're welcome to stay for supper." David wondered where his dad was. Probably out and about on cross country skis or snowshoes, enjoying the weather. David's father had retired from the Vail hotel a few years ago, and now worked as a seniors ski instructor at Copper Mountain. Not bad for an old coot, as he was fond of saying. David had to agree—his dad skied like a twenty-year-old. Had this been an early fall snow, rather than a late spring snow, he would have been hitting the slopes.

"Thanks. I think I will. Do you need help with anything?"

"No, of course not. I'm just going to zap some leftovers. So how have you been?"

"I've been good." He shifted in the soft couch. Memories filled every corner of this house. He looked at the stone hearth and swore he could still feel the crease in his skull where he'd nearly brained himself on it twenty years ago. "We're all settled at the Lakewood office, *Dark Princes II* is ready for release, and *Dark Princes III* is rolling along nicely. Plus I'm looking into doing some educational games."

"Hmm," said Mom. "Still no engagement plans?"

David grinned. "Not since yesterday."

"The wedding thing was last weekend, wasn't it? How did that go?"

David shrugged. "It was fine. A lot of old acquaintances from high school—more than I'd expected, really. Have to admit I felt a little smug, because the group who used to beat me up? Now they want to know what computer to buy."

"Isn't that why you went? To watch them eat crow?"

"Maybe partly... I don't know." He paused, wondering how much he should tell her right now. "Do you remember Tony?"

"Tony Carter?"

"No, no. Tony. Antonytte. Mullin."

"Oh, right. The one who married the James boy." Her eyes brightened with mischief. "The one you used to write the wretched poems about."

David shook his head. Trust Mom to remember the more humiliating moments of his life. He'd forgotten all about those until now—a conveniently selective memory loss on his part. "I don't recall ever showing any of those to you."

"Well, there was the time your teacher found them in with your math homework."

"Oh. Well, never mind that. I saw her at the wedding. She's divorced now."

"Really? I'm sorry to hear that."

"I'm not."

Maddy gave her son a sly look. "Don't tell me your poetic muse is visiting again after ten years."

David pushed himself up from the couch and walked to the fireplace. His high school graduation picture sat on the mantel. God, no wonder she'd snubbed him. He'd definitely improved with age, if he did say so himself.

"Not that exactly. It's just..." He wasn't completely sure what he wanted to ask. "Do you think it's possible for someone to be in love—I mean really in love—at fifteen or sixteen?"

"Your father and I fell in love in high school."

"Yeah, but it was mutual. Tony never would give me the time of day. Now..."

"Now what?"

"It feels different."

Maddy eyed her son intently. "What exactly happened at the wedding?"

David shrugged. "We talked, we danced, her car died, she stayed in my guest room, and today we had lunch. And I asked her to dinner on Friday."

Maddy considered. "If she says yes, you can assume she's no longer just using you for algebra."

David rolled his eyes. Mom could hold a grudge like nobody David knew.

"But what if none of this is real?" he asked. "What if it's just some stupid holdover crush from high school?"

Maddy was silent a moment, which put David on his guard. She was mulling something over. Which probably meant David was about to get a lecture. "David, God blessed you with a very efficient brain. Trouble is, you use it for everything. Some things just can't be thought through. You need to cut loose the logic circuits and listen to your heart and soul. That's all that counts."

David frowned. That wasn't what he'd wanted to hear. He wasn't sure he knew how to follow his heart. It had been stomped on too many times following that path. He was so much more comfortable with pie charts and pivot tables.

Then again...

"You mean like following my passion for computer games to form Tachyon?"

Maddy gave a strange smile. "Well, that's probably not a completely fair comparison, but it'll do in a pinch. If she's what you want, then go for it. Otherwise you'll never know."

"Thanks, Mom." He pushed away from the mantel. "I think I'll have that drink now. Preferably something with some kick to it."

Tony went in to work Thursday morning with her backbone freshly starched, ready to spit nails if need be to remedy the situation with her job. She'd done nothing but stew about it the previous afternoon. That was, when she hadn't been thinking about David.

The office manager was in, drinking a cup of tea and reading e-mail. She was a heavyset but utterly immaculate woman. After only three days on the job, Tony had determined Ms. Thompson's wardrobe was well beyond what she could possibly afford. Tony knew that trick, though. You bought designer patterns, waited for clearance sales at the fabric store, and made the clothes yourself. Tony had been doing it for years.

Tony stepped up to Ms. Thompson's office door, waited until she looked like she'd hit a stopping place, then knocked gently. "Ms. Thompson?"

Ms. Thompson looked up, carefully plucked eyebrows lifted. "Antonytte? What can I do for you?"

"I need to talk to you about my job."

Ms. Thompson gestured to an extra chair sitting near her desk. "Have a seat."

When Tony had settled, Ms. Thompson swiveled toward her, bestowing her full attention. "How can I help you?"

Tony summoned the courage she'd woken up with this morning and gave it a moment to soak through her. "I was told this was to be a full-time data entry position, not a part-time job as a filing clerk. I really need to get more work, or I'm going to have to ask my agency for another assignment."

Ms. Thompson studied her, evaluating. "I see." Her computer beeped, indicating incoming mail, and she gave it a sidelong glance. "The data entry position was filled the day before you came on board. Unfortunately there was a miscommunication with your agency. I'm sorry you were given the wrong information."

"Why wasn't I told this on the first day?"

"Because I had hoped to keep you on. I really need a full-time assistant, but my supervisor has yet to approve the request."

Tony's heart sank. She would have to get a new assignment, which meant a new routine, going to another building, getting acquainted with new people... She was beginning to hate the constant adjustments and transitions. But she couldn't stay here. Part time just wouldn't pay her rent, or her tuition. Things were working out fairly well so far, but she needed a certain number of hours through the temp agency to qualify for their health insurance plan in addition to keeping the cash flow where she needed it to be.

Ms. Thompson had been thinking, though, and apparently had an idea.

"I might be able to arrange something for you, Antonytte. I have a project here that's been put aside, and I know the CEO would be pleased if we could get it underway again. How fast do you type?"

"One-twenty on a good day."

"Great. Now, all this research material was handwritten and needs to be transcribed..."

So Tony spent the next few hours typing from a stack of blue notebooks, deciphering a lazy male scrawl. The material had to do with environmental concerns, and Tony found some of it interesting until she passed into her typist's trance, where she was aware of the text as only a blur of letters. Once she hit that point, her mind was free to wander.

It wandered straight to David. Not surprising, really—he'd been heavy in her thoughts of late. She only had twelve hours or so to decide if she would meet him for a second date. Or maybe this should be the first date, since yesterday's lunch had only been repayment for the use of his guest room. Or maybe it wouldn't be a date at all—just a couple of old high school acquaintances getting together for dinner.

Why not a date, though? Her thoughts changed tracks abruptly. She visualized David's big, gentle hands caressing her face, heard his steady voice saying things she'd always wished Rudy would say...

"Antonytte?"

Tony jumped, fingers stuttering on the keyboard. She put a hand to her chest to keep her heart from leaping out. Ms. Thompson stood next to her desk, trying not to smile.

"I'm sorry. I didn't mean to startle you."

Tony swallowed, collecting herself. "It's okay. I just completely lose track of everything when I'm typing."

"Probably why you can type so fast. I don't think I've ever seen fingers fly like that."

Smiling, Tony self-consciously tangled her hands together in her lap. "Thanks," she said, not sure she meant it. Yes, she could type fast, but that wasn't all she could do.

Ms. Thompson looked at her a moment, seeming to consider, then took a quick breath. "I'm afraid I have some bad news."

Tony's heart lurched. "What...what kind of bad news?"

"I spoke to my supervisor, and even though the CEO wants this project taken care of, I'm afraid we can't sustain another full-time person. In fact, I've been asked to cut you back to three half-days a week. I'm terribly sorry."

"So am I," said Tony, her voice wooden. She barely heard her own words. Why did this hurt so much? She knew it wasn't personal, and so did Ms. Thompson. "Then I'm afraid I'll only be able to stay until I can find another position."

"I understand." She touched Tony's shoulder. "I'm really sorry. I think under other conditions we might have been able to find a permanent position for you here."

And instead you're firing me after three days. "It's all right, Ms. Thompson. I know you tried to help." She set her fingers back on the keyboard. Ms. Thompson nodded and went back to her work.

Great. Now she'd have to go through the whole job-hunting process all over again. Why she put herself through this, she didn't know.

No, she did know. She stuck with the temp agency because they gave her the flexibility to keep up with her course schedule. If she needed a few days off to study for exams, she could take it. If she wanted a month off in the summer, she could do that, too. She'd even been with the agency long enough she could get paid for some of her time off, and they provided health insurance if she maintained her hours.

Tony's fingers began to fly again, tickety tickety tickety, as under her breath she chanted, "I hate this stinking job, I hate this stinking job…"

Chapter Five

"Kill the orc! Kill the orc!"

David winced as Rich shouted in his ear. Frustrated, he banged the mouse on the mouse pad, then pulled the keyboard drawer out from under the desk and started banging the space bar, then the return key. All to no avail—the orc hammered one last blow on his Aethelfried, and she died in an ignominious sloughing of geometric shapes.

Rich smacked him on the back of the head.

"Why didn't you kill the damned orc?"

"Ow!" Rubbing the back of his head, David swiveled his chair toward his business partner, co-owner of Tachyon Software and head of the art department. Rich's blondish hair was standing on end where he'd been yanking on it during the admittedly frustrating game. "I didn't kill the damned orc because the damned software glitched out on me again."

"I thought you fixed that."

"I thought I did too." With a sigh, he shut off the game. "I give up. I'm turning it over to the programming team. Maybe they can figure it out. How are the graphics coming?"

"They're not."

David looked at him, surprised not only by Rich's words, but by the annoyance in his tone. Game-related histrionics aside, Rich was one of the most laid-back people David knew. "What do you mean they're not?"

Rich pointed to the large folder he'd tossed on David's desk when he'd come in about an hour ago. "That's really what I intended to talk to you about, before you distracted me with your incompetent game play."

David picked up the folder and paged through the pictures. The two artists working on *Dark Princes III* had put together sketches of the game's lead characters. David shook his head. He had a very clear idea of what Aethelfried should look like, and this was not it.

"What's with the breasts?" he said. "She doesn't need a sword—she can stab the orcs to death with these things. And the rest of her—good Lord, she looks like some mutant offspring of Vin Diesel and Lady Gaga." He paged through to another picture. "Cripes, even the horses are on steroids." He tossed the folder to the desk and fixed Rich with a look that bordered on anger. "What the hell is going on?"

"Luz left, that's what's going on." Rich sank into the extra chair beside David's desk. "These guys are geniuses at computer animation, but Luz was the brains behind the designs. She just had an instinct for what was right."

David harrumphed. "Well, I hope one of those elephants she's painting in Kenya steps on her." Not that he meant it, of course. Luz had always been a free spirit, and the wildlife paintings would generate profits for charity.

But that didn't solve David's problem. "We need to get another artist on this project, and quick. If we don't get the designs finalized for at least Aethelfried and the two companions by the first of the month, we're going to have to push the release date back. And I really don't want to do that."

A soft knock sounded on the office door, and Nancy put her head in, looking like someone might bite her.

"I'm very sorry, Mr. Peterson, but you have a phone call. It's a Ms. Mullin. You told me you wanted to take it no matter what?"

David jerked upright, causing Rich to eye him with alert interest. "Yes. Yes, absolutely. Thank you, Nancy." He lifted the receiver to his ear, finger poised above the appropriate button. "And call me David!" But Nancy was already gone. David punched the button. "Hello?"

"Hi, David. It's Tony."

"Hi, Tony. How are you doing?" He glanced at Rich, who mouthed, "Tony?" David waved him off.

"I'm not so great. I'm starting a new temp assignment on Monday."

"I thought you just started a new temp assignment?"

"I did. Long story. Look, about tonight..." She trailed off as if collecting herself, and David's heart constricted. She was going to bow out.

"Look, if you're busy—"

"No, no, it's not that." He heard her take a breath. "I think I can come, but I want you to tell me something."

David looked again at Rich, who seemed quite absorbed in his eavesdropping. "Yes?"

"I just don't know how you meant this. I mean, if you intended it to be a date or what. But I'd really like to just keep it social, okay?"

David made a face at Rich, causing Rich to lift his eyebrows. "I didn't necessarily intend it as a date. Just time to catch up, you know."

"Okay. I just wanted to be sure we were on the same wavelength, that's all. I'm sorry if that was too forward."

"No, no. It's best we get these things out in the open. I've got some things to finish up here, so I should be by about seven. Is that okay?"

"That's fine."

"I'll see you then."

He hung up the phone. Rich leaned back in his chair, folding his hands behind his head. "You did so intend it for a date."

"Damn straight I did. And it will be before the night's over." He wasn't going to let a little thing like Tony's lack of self-confidence derail his plans.

"Well, if it doesn't work out, give her my number." He rose and picked up his folder, preparing to leave. "But only if she's got breasts you could impale an orc with."

For the fourth time, Tony pulled down her carefully constructed French twist. Her hair refused to lay quite the way she wanted it to, and for some reason it looked streaky today.

She rolled and twisted and poked and adjusted and reapplied her big silver claw clip. There. That was at least acceptable. She coated the arrangement lightly with hair spray. Then, looking in the mirror, she realized her mouth looked crooked. With a sigh, she pulled her lipstick back out.

A small part of her mind wondered why she was going to so much trouble for something that wasn't a date. If she intended to see David on a purely social basis, then what in the world did it matter what she looked like?

The only answer she had was that it *did* matter, and that didn't bode well for any of her David-related resolutions.

She glanced at the clock, wondering if it was too late to call and cancel. It was. He should be here in about fifteen minutes, which meant he had probably just left his office.

Lipstick adjusted, Tony made a few last tweaks to her clothes. She'd forgotten to ask if she should dress up, so she'd erred on the side of caution, choosing a dark lavender linen suit and white silk blouse. She'd found the blouse on a clearance rack, and she'd made the suit herself. More than one person had mistaken it for a designer outfit. She looked good, she thought—not too formal, not too casual. And it was comfortable too, which was always a plus.

There wasn't much else she could do, she decided, so she went into the living room to wait.

As she settled onto the couch, she looked around her, wondering what David would think of this room. She'd put a lot of thought into the room's arrangement and decoration, hoping to engineer a good first impression. She kept a small cabinet full of carefully dusted knickknacks next to the medium-size TV. They had been chosen to look like a set, even though she'd purchased most of them at thrift stores.

Above the TV and above the couch were watercolors of her own creation, abstract pictures that picked up all the colors of the room. Counted cross-stitch designs, also Tony's originals, graced the small, predominately green kitchen. All mixed traditional with a modern twist.

By contrast, David's house had been sleekly modern, with the black lacquer furniture and the electronics equipment that seemed more a part of the decor than functional units. She hoped he would like something about her apartment.

Why does it matter? Shaking her head in mild disgust at herself, Tony went to the kitchen and mixed up a pitcher of instant iced tea. She had just quartered a lemon and dropped the pieces into the pitcher when her doorbell rang.

Unaccountable nervousness twisted Tony's stomach. Quickly, she rinsed lemon juice from her hands, deposited the tea in the refrigerator, and hurried to the door.

Again, David surprised her. It was as if her mind reverted to his high school image when she was away from him, so that every time she saw him she had to peel that veneer away. The gray eyes and the ridiculously kissable mouth threw her off, as did the width of his shoulders under his trench coat. And he was so tall...

"Hi," he said, smiling.

"Hi." Tony collected herself, hoping he hadn't noticed her little lapse into near shock. "Come on in."

He stepped into the apartment, coattails lifting a bit behind him. The day had been warm, but Tony was sure the temperature had dropped fifteen or twenty degrees since sunset. He wore dark blue trousers, she noticed, with a casual shirt and a tie featuring Obi-Wan Kenobi—the original, not the Obi-Wan from the sequels—so her outfit wasn't too far off.

"This is a nice place," he said. "I like the paintings. Where did you get them?"

"Oh, I did those myself."

He looked at her in surprise. "Really? They're wonderful."

"Thanks." Praise always flustered her, his even more so. "So, um...do we have to leave right away, or what's the schedule?"

David looked at his watch. "We didn't need reservations, and the place isn't usually very crowded, so there's no real hurry."

"Where are we going?"

"An Italian place—that is, if that's okay with you."

"It's fine. I love Italian." She picked up her purse, then realized she'd have to put it down to get her coat on. She put it back down and went to the closet. David was still looking at the paintings and so wouldn't have noticed her faux pas.

"Did you ever think about going into commercial art?"

Tony pulled her coat from the hanger, feeling herself tense involuntarily. "Yes, I did."

"What made you decide not to?" He was looking at her now, his gray eyes carrying nothing but curiosity. Tony couldn't quite meet them.

"A lot of things." She shrugged into her coat and picked up her purse again. "How was your day?"

He twitched an eyebrow at her change of subject. "I don't want to talk about work."

"I don't want to talk about art."

She opened the door. David followed her out, his hand brushing her back. All her skin went warm at the touch. Such graceful hands, she'd noticed. She loved to watch them move...

Good grief, where had that come from? David stepped ahead of her, leading the way down the stairs to the parking lot.

"What *can* we talk about, then?" he asked. His tan trench coat lay smooth against his wide shoulders, hugging his back, then falling free just above his waist to sway as he walked. Tony couldn't remember ever having found a trench coat so alluring before.

"I'm studying for finals in my accounting class," she said, barely registering the words. "I've got a good chance of getting an A if I do well on the exams."

He had driven the Mercedes. The top was down, the passenger seat scattered with CDs. He walked around to the passenger door and opened it for her, then bent past her to pick up the CDs and put them on the dashboard.

"That's great," he said, then, after he'd rounded the car and slid into the driver's seat, "I took some accounting in college..."

The conversation meandered over neutral territory until they reached the restaurant. It was a small, locally owned establishment. The name sounded familiar. Tony vaguely remembered seeing a review in the *Denver Post*, but she couldn't remember what the article had said.

Inside, they were enveloped by a homey atmosphere and the smell of garlic and oil. Tony's mouth began to water. As David had said, there were only a few people waiting, and in a few minutes they were seated.

"This place kind of reminds me of the Junior prom," David said after they'd ordered. "Remember? They did that Venice theme and made the teachers dress like gondoliers?"

Tony smiled hesitantly. "And I refused to dance with you."

David shrugged. "It could have been worse. My date could have stood me up. Oh, wait—I didn't have one."

She narrowed her eyes at him, trying to judge his expression. He seemed to have deadpan down to a science. "You're trying to make me feel guilty, aren't you?"

That drew a wry grin out of him. "No. Not at all."

"You act like it was a good memory for you."

"It's the past, Tony. It's over. There's enough distance now that I can look at it and laugh. Or, you know, at least not throw up."

Tony wondered if she would ever be able to do that. To look back at the humiliation she'd experienced when Rudy had forced her away, cheated on her, finally left her, and not feel that horrible, wrenching twist in the pit of her stomach. And now her memories were folding over themselves, matching what Rudy had done to her to what she done to David, and that twist took on a new dimension. How badly had she hurt him back then? She didn't even know. She hadn't even cared.

Suddenly, she put her face in her hands, collecting herself while the wrenching feeling tried to take her breath away.

David leaned toward her. "Tony, are you okay?"

The waiter arrived then to take their drink orders, and Tony took advantage of the interruption both to gather her dangerously drifting emotions and avoid his question. By the time the waiter had jotted down the information on his notepad and departed, she was fairly certain she wouldn't burst into tears in the middle of the restaurant.

"I'm sorry." At first she thought she was apologizing for her near emotional outburst. Then she realized that wasn't what she meant at all. "I'm sorry I treated you the way I did. All I ever thought about was myself. All I considered was that I was the cheerleader and Rudy was the handsome quarterback. And I should've paid more attention to you because, dammit, you were *nice*."

She picked up her water glass and drank, swallowing still-lurking tears with the icy water. "You still are nice," she managed, "and I don't understand why you'd even give me the time of day, much less take me to dinner."

She finally managed to look at him. He was watching her, his expression carefully neutral.

After a moment, he asked, "Why did you go to the wedding?"

The question surprised her. She picked up her water glass again, moving it in front of her. "Julia asked me. She wanted to have the same bridesmaid."

David nodded. "I went for revenge." At her surprised expression, he nodded again. "That's right, revenge. Against all the 'popular' kids who snubbed me and beat me up, and against that idiot Eric Lockham who used to steal my lunch money. Then I saw you there. It never occurred to me you'd be there—I don't know why. I mean, just about everybody else from our graduating class was. Made me wonder why the hell Julia didn't just plan a reunion." He waved the thought away. "I saw you. And you were...you're..." He stopped, closed his eyes as if gathering his thoughts. "Everything I felt for you back then—I was sure I'd outgrown it. That it was just a high school thing. Those things happen. They're natural. But when I saw you again, all those feelings came back except...except *more*. They weren't a kid's feelings anymore."

Tony looked away again. She didn't know what to say to him. Didn't know what to do with any of this information.

"And when I found out you'd left Rudy—I decided I'd be damned if I was going to let you get away without finding out if there could be something between us." He took a slow breath and looked at her. "Now do you understand? Or do you just want to get up and leave?"

Tony swallowed a sudden, sticky thickness in her throat. In all her time with Rudy, she'd never heard such a raw declaration of emotion. The small, secret affection she'd felt beginning to grow for David opened up warmly within her.

"If I leave," she said, "I won't get any dessert."

David smiled, and the waiter arrived with their meals.

By apparent mutual consent, the conversation shifted to lighter topics through the meal, but after a time the subject fell on Tony's marriage.

"I was really surprised you two had broken up," David said. "You always seemed so happy."

"I *was* happy," Tony said. She sipped her wine. It was an excellent brand, something she never would have ordered herself. "Mostly because I didn't know any better."

"Why did you leave him?"

Tony shrugged. Only Julia knew all the sordid details. Automatically, she supplied her standard story.

"Rudy drove a truck. Still does, as far as I know. He was gone a lot. Eventually, we drifted apart." She paused and took a drink, wondering why the story felt so strange today. Usually she could breeze through the half-lies and almost truths. When she resumed, she found herself unable to meet David's eyes. "The separations were what kept us together, actually. I assumed we could work things out, if we gave it enough time."

"But it didn't work?"

Tony took another drink. When she opened her mouth again to speak, the story came out.

"While he was gone, everything seemed so much easier. Like he could come home one day and we'd just figure it all out. But then I was sent home from work early one day and found him in bed with a dental hygienist. And she was *not* cleaning his teeth."

David grimaced. "That had to have been rough."

Tony nodded. "I found out later that he'd had at least five other affairs while we were married."

She cupped her hand under the bowl of the wineglass, not lifting it, just feeling its coolness and its weight against her palm. Why had this suddenly come out of her? And why did she feel the need to tell David more? When had she become comfortable enough not to assume he would hurt her?

"I spent a long time wondering what I did wrong," she went on. "It made me feel so…little. Worthless. Then I realized it was Rudy who was little and worthless."

David reached across the table. Tony's free hand lay palm down on the table between them. Gently, his fingers traced the veins on the back of her hand. A simple touch, but Tony's heart began a rapid tattoo, and desire filled her so fast and hot she could hardly breathe past it. The intensity of it frightened her. She looked up at him and was surprised by the mildness in his eyes.

"Anyone," he said quietly, "who would treat you like that is a fool."

Tony could say nothing. She could only look at him, seeing the boy, seeing the man, and wanting him so fiercely she ached with it. He laid his hand flat against hers and squeezed it, breaking the spell. Tony managed a weak smile and drew her hand away, giving it refuge in her lap.

After a time, they spoke again, but she was only barely aware of what was said. It was all over. From this moment on, all David-related resolutions were null and void.

Chapter Six

Through the rest of the meal, through dessert, they talked and laughed. Tony felt more at ease than she had in a long time.

As they meandered to the car, she wondered if she'd had too much wine. David's arm slipped around her waist for a few steps, then withdrew as he opened the car door for her. Tony remembered how it had felt to stand wrapped in warmth and music and his arms. The thought led to the image of a more intimate embrace. Thankful for the darkness, Tony lowered her head over her purse as David took his place on the driver's side.

"You all right?" he said, putting the key in the ignition.

She looked up at him, wayward thoughts under control again. "I'm fine. Just too much wine, I think. I don't drink that often."

He smiled. "Guess I'd better take you home and put you to bed, then."

Tony's breath caught. So much for controlling wayward thoughts. He didn't seem to realize what he'd said. Maybe she *had* had too much wine.

The ride home was quiet, music from the radio filling the small car. When they arrived at Tony's building, and stood in the parking lot, David put out a bent elbow. Tony looped her arm through it. The cool, dry night air stirred her hair where it had fallen down around her face.

"Let's go for a walk," she said.

David looked surprised but willing. "Where?"

"Just around the complex. It's nice and quiet." She looked up at the sky. "And it's such a clear night. Look at the stars." She tugged at his arm. "Come on."

He followed without protest as she led the way along the sidewalk to the back part of the complex. Behind the apartment buildings stretched a wide, dark field. A chain-link fence separated it from the paved, well-lit world of the apartments.

"What's this?" David asked, eyeing the fence. An electrical wire ran across the top. Tony took her emergency penlight from her purse and directed the beam at the fence.

"It used to be a horse pasture, but the guy with the horses moved away. Nobody's lived here for a couple of months. The wire's dead." She handed the flashlight to David and deftly put herself over the four-foot fence. "Come on. The view's great from out here."

Turning back toward David, she could barely see his bemused expression in the bobbling light. He took hold of the fence, though, and a few minutes later stood next to her. "Do you take all your dates out here?"

"Yeah, sure, all of them." Tony took the flashlight back. Her head was light with the wine and maybe with David. She wanted to see stars. Reaching back, she caught David's hand in hers and dragged him after her. "Come on."

Zigzagging the beam of the flashlight, she managed to find the grassy knoll where she had sat two weeks ago, watching a meteor shower. She normally wouldn't have been so bold, but she'd never seen a meteor shower before, and it had seemed fairly safe to be out here even alone, since it was fenced-off private property.

She certainly wouldn't have been so bold tonight, if not for the wine and the strange spirit that seemed to have taken her over. She pulled David to the top of the little hill, sat down and turned off the flashlight.

"There," she said. "Look."

In the starlight and the nearly full moon, she could see his smile. Then, to her surprise, he flopped down on his back in the grass. In spite of the snowfall at Eagle Creek, there'd been very little precipitation in Denver or the suburbs, and the temperatures had been much more springlike. Typical—the altitude played havoc with the temperatures in the mountains, and the mountains themselves played havoc with the weather systems.

For a moment David was silent, staring at the great wash of stars. Tony craned her neck to follow his gaze, then lay down beside him. Chill seeped quickly from the ground, through her coat and suit, into her skin. Above her the black sky stared at her with a million tiny eyes.

"The Milky Way," David said, his voice a murmur in the breeze. He didn't bother to point. "The Pleiades. Cassiopeia. The Big Dipper."

"You can probably see these stars every night from your deck," Tony said as the North Star winked at her.

"I can." She felt him shift, turning toward her. "But it's not the same."

Tony fixed her eyes to the sky. Her heartbeat galloped in her throat, and warmth filled her in spite of the chill. She didn't want to look at him. Something powerful lay in the air between them, and if she turned, she would acknowledge it. Lying there, feeling what lay just beyond her grasp if she would only take it, she realized she had never known anything quite like this before.

Terrified, eager, she turned toward him.

His face was still, and in the darkness she couldn't see the expression in his eyes. He lifted a hand to cup her cheek, the tips of his fingers grazing her cheekbone. A soft sound came from Tony's throat. David leaned toward her. She answered with a movement of her own, and they met somewhere in the middle.

His kiss was gentle, almost reverent at first; then his arm went around her, drawing her to him. His soft mouth moved against hers, his tongue traced her lips. She parted her lips, and he moved within her. He tasted of coffee. In the darkness and starlight, she seemed to melt into him, her tongue sliding against his, her breath and his breath mingling between them.

After a time, he drew away, and Tony was surprised to see that the stars hadn't moved.

"So much for keeping it social," she murmured, though she could barely find her voice.

He smiled, looking not at all repentant. "Should I take it back?"

"Please do."

There were no excuses this time. She couldn't dismiss it as a fluke or an accident, because this time she'd asked for it. Again he closed the distance between them; again she marveled at the soft beauty of his sensual mouth. The kiss came soft this time, almost chaste. Tony had never been kissed like this before, with such restrained, aching tenderness. There was something to be said, she supposed, for letting love ferment for a decade…

She broke away from him as quickly as if he'd hurt her, shocked by the betrayal of her thoughts. Sitting up, she pressed her hand to her mouth, feeling on it the dampness of his. The spell he had cast on her had fallen in pieces on the grass, and reality had her heart beating so hard she couldn't think. David sat up next to her, concern etching his face.

"What's wrong?"

Tony swallowed. Why was she crying? She pushed away from David, to her feet.

"Nothing," she said, but her voice betrayed her with a lurch. "I'm fine."

Folding her arms across her chest, she started back toward the apartment building. This had gotten entirely out of hand. What was she thinking, dragging him out into the middle of a horse pasture to look at the stars? Not to mention kissing him.

"Tony..." His voice followed her on the chilly breeze; then she heard his footsteps behind her, and his hand touched her arm. "Tony, what is it?"

"Nothing." She kept walking, stopping just short of shrugging off his hand. "I just... I think I had too much to drink." She almost careened into the fence. For a moment, she stood staring at it blankly, unable to remember what she was supposed to do.

"Here." David's hands circled her waist. "Let me help you."

"No!" She jerked out of his grasp and scrambled over the fence herself, barely registering the sound of a seam giving way.

On the other side of the fence, back in the lighted parking lot, she managed to stop. David caught up a moment later, but she didn't turn toward him. She expected him to touch her again, but he didn't.

"Talk to me, Tony."

Hearing his soft, familiar voice, she closed her eyes and saw the David Peterson she'd thought she knew—tall and awkward, pushing heavy glasses up his long nose as he patiently explained simultaneous equations. As hard as it had been for her, as many times as he had to repeat examples, explanations, exercises, not once had he ever told her she was stupid. When she'd been on the verge of tears trying to sort out the variables and solutions, he just waited her out, patted her shoulder awkwardly once or twice and then tried again. Over and over, until she figured it out. Picturing that face, she realized the terrible truth—that, even then, when she had used him and snubbed him and ridiculed him behind his back—even then, she had felt something for him. Something warm and comfortable.

Unable to hold the tears back any longer, she turned to see the man David had become, the man she suddenly wanted with everything she was. Cheeks wet, heart aching, she took his hand in both of hers, then let it go. As much as she wanted to reach out and accept what she knew he was offering, she couldn't. She was so, so afraid. Of breaking herself again. Of breaking him.

"David, I'm sorry."

She turned, and ran up the stairs.

David watched her go, wondering what he'd done wrong. It should have been easy, once all the facts were out on the table. Instead, things seemed to have veered out of his control. Finally he went back to the car and drove home. He couldn't do much at this point other than withdraw, regroup and formulate a new plan.

The trek up into the mountains had never seemed so long. In the middle of Kenosha Pass, he pulled over to the side of the road, got out and lay down on the hood.

The sky spread huge above him. It was like lying in a bowl—the wide-open fields that spread for a few miles in either direction before butting up against stark, snow-covered mountains, and above it all the curve of deep, deep sky. In the complete darkness of the mountains, the stars were even more vivid than they had been in Tony's field. The Milky Way made a great gash of white in the blackness, like a wound or a flow of tears.

He wasn't sure how much time had passed when the Park County Sheriff's car pulled in behind him. David rolled from the hood as the deputy approached. The light from his headlights washed across David, breaking the spell of the darkness.

"Good evening, Officer," David said. The deputy looked to be a bit younger than David and understandably leery of a man lying on top of a Mercedes at one in the morning.

"Is there a problem?" the deputy asked.

David grinned grimly. "Not with the car." At the deputy's skeptical look, he offered, "Driver's license and registration?"

"That would be nice," said the deputy.

David pulled his wallet from his hip pocket and surrendered both items. Leaning against the car, he waited while the deputy ran a check.

"That's a very nice car, Mr. Peterson," he said as he returned. He handed back David's license and registration cards. "So what *are* you doing out here?"

"I just stopped to look at the stars." He repocketed the wallet. "Are you married, Officer?"

The deputy nodded. "Five years last week."

"Do women make any sense to you at all?"

The deputy laughed. "Not one damn bit." He touched the brim of his hat. "I'd best get going. Now, it's not illegal to park by the side of the road, but I have to say it's unwise at this time of night."

"Yeah, I should be going anyway."

The deputy departed, and David followed him for a few miles, until the sheriff's car turned off onto a side road. David kept driving into the long dark.

He could have looked at the stars off his deck instead of lying on his car by the side of the road, but he'd needed the vast silence and the sense that he was alone with the sky. A few pieces of the puzzle that was Tony had seemed to mesh, though there was still a great deal he didn't understand. He'd puzzle it out, though. He wasn't even close to ready to drop this. Setbacks didn't set him back—they just made him that much more determined to move forward.

At home, he changed clothes and tried to work but couldn't concentrate. He tried to watch TV, found an old Humphrey Bogart movie he'd never quite managed to watch all the way through. When it was over, he couldn't remember what had happened.

As he sat trying to make his mind blank, it occurred to him that, although he'd intended to strip the sheets off the bed in the guest room, he hadn't gotten around to it. He hadn't even poked his nose in the room since Tony had spent the night. This was as good a time as any to take care of it, he supposed.

Opening the door to the guest room, he froze for a moment. He felt suddenly as if Tony was in the room with him, and it took a moment for him to realize why. It was the smell. She had worn perfume that night, he remembered, and the smell, soft and delicate as rose petals, hung in the air. He went to the bed and touched the pillow, then lifted it to his face and breathed. With a smile, he laid the pillow back down.

Good God, you're besotted. He shook his head at himself in bemusement. This was worse than high school. Worse because, as an adult, he should be able to deal with these things more adroitly. Worse because the responses were no longer those of a boy but those of a man, and he had a feeling they would not leave him easily. He only hoped he wouldn't have to find out.

He sat on the bed and looked at the room, wondering if she'd left anything else of herself behind. Not that it was likely, but if she'd forgotten a glove or something, it would be a good excuse to see her again.

Apparently, though, she'd picked up after herself fairly thoroughly. Except for one thing. The pile of paper he'd given her that night lay on the nightstand. David reached over to pick it up. He could put the blank pages back in the printer.

He stood, preparing to take the paper to his office. But as he turned the stack over, he discovered the sheets weren't blank at all. Tony had simply turned the pages over, pictures down. And the pictures... Slowly, David sat, staring.

"Oh my God." It was all he could say. He flipped from page to page, transfixed.

The sketches were rough, but it didn't matter. Here in his hand, rendered in black ballpoint, he held the exact image of Aethelfried.

The wind whipped through Tony's hair, making her jacket billow behind her. After only half an hour on Rollerblades, her legs burned, but she knew that would subside shortly. She'd be sore tomorrow, though—this was her first outing this spring. Next to her and a bit behind, Julia glided. She ice skated through the winter and so was in rather better shape.

"What a gorgeous day," Julia said.

Tony couldn't argue. The breeze was slightly chilly, but the sun glared down hot enough to make up for it. Tony had slathered on sunscreen before they went out, having learned from experience that high-altitude air, the sun and her fair skin didn't mix well. And, though she hadn't yet decided if she was going to see David again, she knew for certain she didn't want to do it with her nose peeling.

"So," Julia said, skating faster to catch up with Tony. "Fill me in. Last I knew what was going on, you got stranded at the community center."

Tony nodded, concentrating as she matched her pace to Julia's. They hadn't had a chance to talk since Tony had left the message on Julia's answering machine, so, given recent developments, Tony had jumped at Julia's offer to drive down for the day. It was high time, Julia said, that her husband get some quality time with their three children.

"Apparently, the alternator died on the car," Tony said. "I couldn't get it repaired until the next day."

"So what did you do?"

Tony looked straight ahead. The trail curved here, giving them a spectacular view of the Morrison hogback. Beyond the sharp-edged ridge jutted the sienna stones of Red Rocks amphitheater and the surrounding park.

"I went home with David."

Julia's skates made a stuttering sound against the concrete as she lost her rhythm for a moment.

"You went *home* with *David?*"

Tony dared a glance back at her friend. Julia's face was alight with shock.

"I didn't have much choice. You had to go home to take care of the baby, and the only people around by then were the cheerleading squad and some of Rudy's old football buddies. And David. He said he had a guest room." She paused, negotiating a curve in the trail. "Any port in a storm, I guess."

"I guess." Julia drifted ahead of her, shaking her head. "So what happened?"

Tony shrugged. "Nothing, really. I got to see the advance copy of *Dark Princes II*. Got a look at *Dark Princes III* too."

Julia cast her a narrow-eyed look. "Did you get a look at anything else?"

"Well, he has a pretty darn big"—she changed her stride again, matching Julia's—"house."

Julia grinned wryly. "Well, you know what they say about men with big houses."

The conversation came to a halt for a few minutes as they adjusted to pass a group of people on foot. When they were side by side again, Julia said, "So that's it? End of story?"

"Not really. I saw him on Wednesday and again on Friday."

Julia lifted her hands in surrender. "That's it. I can't concentrate on skating if you're going to drop bombshells like that on me. We're going to have to stop."

They rolled off the concrete trail and flopped down on the dry grass. The ground was dry as well. They'd gotten some rain just after the snow, but the thirsty earth had devoured it. Julia pulled off her safety helmet and shook her dark hair free. "All right. Tell me the story."

Tony pulled off her own helmet, scrubbing away the ring of sweat around her hairline.

"Okay. The first date was just so I could thank him for putting me up. The Friday date was purely optional."

Julia nodded wisely. "I see. He's still got a thing for you."

109

Tony peered up at the cloudless sky. "I think it might be worse than that. I think I might still have a thing for him."

Julia's jaw dropped. "I didn't think you ever *had* a thing for him."

"I didn't either..." Tony lurched to her feet, picking up her helmet. Suddenly, the unsaid words seemed to be choking her. She'd said things she hadn't meant to say, and she didn't want to try to explain something to Julia that she truly didn't understand herself. "I...I'm sorry. Never mind. I don't really want to talk about it. Let's just skate."

Julia grabbed her by the ankle. "No way, girl. You sit your hiney down here and talk to me."

Tony considered, then dropped her helmet and sat back down. "I don't know if I can."

"Try."

Tony pulled her knees up and put her head down. The sun burned the back of her neck as her hair fell over her shoulders. Julia tapped her on the back. She'd carried a pair of water bottles on a belt at her waist and held one out to Tony. Tony lifted her head and took the water.

"It's hard for you to talk about things like this, isn't it?" Julia said.

"Well, I haven't had much practice. My mother never really wanted to hear about anything too deep, and Rudy was never much for profound conversation."

Julia snorted. "Rudy was never much for any kind of conversation."

"Rudy wasn't all bad." She had no idea why she was defending him, except that there had been a few good moments.

Julia shook her head. "No, you've got that wrong. Rudy was no good."

Tony didn't comment. There was no point arguing against the truth. "So how do I know David's any different?"

"Oh, please. David and Rudy are as different as..." Julia broke off. "Wait a minute. Why would it even matter to you unless..."

Tony put her face in her hands and nodded.

"Good grief, you act like it's the end of the world. There are certainly much worse things that could happen to you than falling for David Peterson. I mean, he's rich, he's handsome, and he's been crazy for you for ages." She poked Tony with the water bottle again. Tony looked up and took it.

"Everybody keeps saying that. That he had a crush on me in high school. He never had a crush on me in high school. He was just...I don't know."

Julia tipped her head back to face the sky as if seeking divine intervention. Her dark, curly hair tumbled over her shoulders. "My God, Tony. Everybody in our class knew David had a crush on you. Except you."

Tony took a moment to absorb that. It didn't feel very good, for several reasons. First, because she'd never taken him seriously back then. Second, because of the implications for what was happening between them now.

"But if it's just an...infatuation..." she protested.

"If it were just an infatuation, it wouldn't have lasted this long." Julia eyed Tony narrowly as Tony took a drink. "Did I ever tell you I used to have a crush on Danny Malone?"

Tony's eyes widened, and she nearly sputtered out the water in her mouth. "No way."

Julia nodded solemnly, her sweaty hair sticking to her forehead. "I wanted him desperately. The way he used to play that trumpet... Anyway, I was looking forward to seeing him at the reunion, just to see if the flame was still there. And I did see him. He's quite a handsome man still, and very nice, but there was no flame anymore."

"None?"

"Not a flicker."

Tony shook her head. "But it's not really a fair test. I mean, you've been married for ages to a really great guy. You have no reason to feel sparks for another man."

Julia snorted. "I'm married, not dead. Believe me, I've felt sparks for other men more times than I could count. But I've outgrown Danny, I guess."

"So you're saying I haven't outgrown David? Or he hasn't outgrown me?"

"Actually, I think you might have just grown into each other."

Tony mulled over that, then finally shook her head. "I don't need another man to try to run my life. I'm doing just fine on my own."

"Tony." Julia's low, serious tone made Tony look at her. "David is not Rudy. Don't let Rudy ruin this for you too." She picked up her helmet. "C'mon. Let's get going, or there's no way we'll get back by noon."

"These are terrific." Rich paged through the pictures, shaking his head in wonderment. "I mean, they're rough, but with some cleaning up, they'd be perfect."

David nodded. "I thought so too." He stretched out, leaning back into the couch cushions. He had invited Rich up to the house for the day, to work out some of the kinks in the *Dark Princes III* prototype. It had seemed like the perfect time to show

Rich the pictures Tony had drawn. He knew she most likely wouldn't take that first step herself—she was dead set on being an accountant for God only knew what reason. David couldn't think of a worse fate for someone with her obvious drive to create art than to be saddled with numbers forever and ever world without end. He could at least get her in the door. Then she'd be on her own to carry it through from there. And then she'd know for certain if art really wasn't the vocation she wanted to pursue. Or at least she would have made a definite decision, rather than making a default decision by not deciding.

"Who did them?"

"Somebody I ran into at that wedding...thing...I went to last weekend. I want you to take them in Monday and run them by the rest of the graphics team. When you're done, I expect them to be as happy about the pictures as you and I are. Then I want you to call the artist and set up an interview."

Rich smiled wryly. "So you're turning this all over to me?"

"Well, I'm planning to spearhead the educational line as soon as *Dark Princes III* is underway, so whoever's hired on will work for you. There are some issues with the artist, like a lack of formal experience, and I want you to see what you can work out." Turning it over to Rich was the best choice too. That way Tony couldn't possibly say he'd manipulated her or was making things happen on her behalf. She'd be on her own, to sink or swim. He was pretty sure that was the way she liked it.

It occurred to him, vaguely, that maybe he should let her know what was going down, that she should expect a phone call. But the voice in his head providing the advice was small, and it sounded like his mother. So he ignored it.

David turned one of the drawings over and wrote "A. Mullin" on the back, as well as Tony's phone number. Rich picked up the papers, stacked them neatly together and put them in his briefcase.

"Okay, boss. Will do."

Tony and Julia Rollerbladed themselves into near exhaustion, then drove to Tony's apartment to take stock of the damage to their feet. Julia called home to see if she was urgently needed.

"Nobody's home," she told Tony. Tony pulled a pitcher of iced tea from the refrigerator and poured a glass. In spite of the quart or so of water she had downed on the trail, she was parched. Julia joined her at the counter to pour her own drink. "They probably went to the park or something. Jim can't handle the kids without taking them somewhere."

"At least he's willing to take them."

They went to the living room and collapsed on the couch. Tony's feet burned. Peeling off her socks, she found a blister on her instep the size of a quarter.

"Good Lord, we're a mess," said Julia, examining her own blistered feet. Propping them on the coffee table, she noticed the yearbooks, which Tony hadn't put back after perusing them last Sunday. Julia leaned forward and paged through the volume from her freshman year.

"There's me!" she announced, pointing herself out in a group shot of the Spanish club. "Look at that god-awful spiky haircut." She laughed. "Mom hated that. She threw such a fit when I dyed it pink too."

Tony peered over her friend's arm at the picture, smiling. "I never could have gotten away with that."

"You were Little Miss Cheerleader. They would have thrown you off the squad if you'd been anything but perky sun-streaked blonde."

Tony leaned back again, sipping her tea. "I never understood how you did it."

"Did what?"

"Stayed on the ins with so many groups. I mean, with me it was the cheerleaders and the football players. I got looked at funny if I talked to anybody outside that group. But you were friends with everybody."

"It's probably because I didn't much care what anybody thought about me. An independent attitude can afford you a certain level of freedom." She turned a few pages. "There's you and Cheryl and Missy and those other three little twerps I never liked."

"As I recall, you called them something stronger than twerps."

"I have to watch my language now. Kids, you know."

"And I don't recall you caring too much for Cheryl and Missy either."

Julia shrugged. "They were okay. I actually like them less now. Cheryl, at least. She never grew out of that clique mentality."

"And I did?"

Julia seemed not to have heard the question. She continued to page through the book.

"Oh, dear," she said after a moment. "He was a nerd poster boy, wasn't he?"

The fondness in Julia's voice surprised Tony. She leaned over to peer at the picture and found affection crowding into her own heart even looking at David's gawky, awkward, old self. She had a sudden urge to pick up the phone and call him, just to hear his voice.

"He was a sweet kid," Julia went on. "A little too serious, though. If he'd been the class clown, I don't think he would've gotten nearly so much flak." She glanced up at Tony. "What's he like now?"

Tony shrugged. She still didn't want to look too closely at her feelings for David. She couldn't figure them out—they were tangled and confused and she didn't have the emotional fortitude to sort through them right now. Not while she was looking at all these memories from the time when she'd made that irrevocable choice that had put her where she was now. "The same, I guess. Smart, sweet, too serious."

"He'd be good for you."

Tony didn't think she'd ever heard Julia sound so sober. She picked up the book and turned a few more pages. "Maybe, maybe not."

"Oh, come on. You need a man like that, somebody who'll prop you up instead of tearing you down."

Tony closed her lips against a flare of anger. On the page she had turned to was a picture of Rudy, with the Junior class. Handsome, chiseled, smiling. He looked like every girl's dream. He'd been hers for a while. Then she woke up.

"I don't need any man at all," she said decisively. "It's just not worth it." She closed the book with a sharp snap and leaned back in the couch to finish her tea.

Chapter Seven

Monday morning, Tony started yet another new job, filling in for an executive secretary who was on vacation. A short assignment, but at least it was guaranteed full-time. They kept her busy too—so busy she thought about David only ten or twelve times the entire first day.

Nevertheless, when she got home and realized he hadn't called, she was disappointed. At least until she reminded herself she didn't want to get involved, not with him or anyone else. Her life was fine just the way it was.

Wednesday night, she dragged in at ten fifteen after her accounting class at the local community college. Her head hurt, and she felt like she had numbers falling out of her ears.

"I hate accounting," she said, slamming her textbook down on the kitchen counter. "Why am I taking accounting? Why do I subject myself to this?"

Repressing an urge to fling the book across the room, she instead stalked into her bedroom. It was late, she was tired, and she was angry for no particular reason. She changed clothes and went back to the living room. As an afterthought, she picked up the phone. It gave the stuttering beep that indicated she had a voice mail.

Tony muttered, hoping it wasn't her mother or even Julia. She was in no mood for the former's pessimistic harping or the latter's cheerfulness. Dreading what she might find, she dialed in.

David's voice spoke from the headset. Tony stilled, anger quieting as she listened.

"Tony, it's David. I'm sorry I didn't call you earlier, but I wasn't sure I should. Anyway, I hope you're doing all right with the new job. If you get a chance, give me a call." He left his number, then added, "I think maybe we need to talk."

We need to talk. Those words had a reputation for presaging disaster, but she didn't think that was what he meant. They needed to talk because they'd kissed, and it had been wonderful. She could still conjure the warmth of his mouth against hers, the after-dinner taste of him. They needed to talk because she'd freaked out and run. They needed to talk because, just maybe, he was worried about her. She'd certainly never heard those words out of Rudy's mouth. When it came to meaningful communication—or any kind of communication, for that matter—he'd belonged to the grunt-and-ignore-it school.

Just the offer to talk made her want to call. She looked at the clock. Ten forty. Had it been anyone else, she would have considered it too late. But she knew David usually worked half the night, so she picked up the phone.

After the fifth ring, she wondered if she'd made a mistake. In the middle of the sixth, she nearly hung up; then he answered. "Hello?"

"Hi. David? It's Tony."

"Tony! Hi!" He sounded genuinely pleased and not at all tired. "I'm sorry I didn't get to the phone quicker. I've got something running on the computer, and I couldn't leave it right away."

"It's okay." She paused. His voice had calmed her already, making her forget the turmoil that had driven her to call in the first place. "If you have to get back to what you were doing—"

"Oh, no, no. It's set now. I'm compiling code. I'm all yours."

"Well... You called earlier?"

"Yeah. I just wanted to see how you were doing. I wasn't sure, though, after what happened..." Tony closed her eyes, remembering his kiss. She must have looked crazed to him, weeping and incoherent, running away at what should have been a tender moment.

"I'm sorry," she said. She sank onto the couch, leaning into the deep cushions. "I wish I..." This was so hard. He was there, waiting and willing to listen, and she could find no words. The silence stretched too long.

"Do you want to talk about it?" David's gentle voice jarred her back.

"No," she said automatically. "I mean—yes, but not over the phone." Maybe if she saw him face-to-face, the words would come. "Maybe...maybe we could get together again."

"Sure. Do you want to meet for lunch? I'm going to be down that way tomorrow and Friday."

"Yes. Yes, that would be good. How about tomorrow? I have to work through lunch on Friday. They're having a special luncheon, and they need me to cover."

"Okay." He paused as if considering. "Can you drop by my office at eleven thirty?"

"Eleven forty-five would be better," she said, wondering what he had in mind.

"Not a problem. I'll meet you out front."

As she hung up the phone, Tony reflected. David had seemed genuinely pleased to hear from her and almost surprised that she'd suggested a date. No, a social get-together, she reminded herself, then sighed. *Forget it. You* know *it's a date.* She wanted it to be a date. She wanted him to kiss her again.

Maybe she even wanted more.

She turned the TV on and fell asleep watching Humphrey Bogart.

Tony was a few minutes late for lunch, having had a load of urgent work dumped on her at eleven. She'd finished it with aplomb, though, and the achievement had not only earned her a compliment from the boss but a sense she'd accomplished something. This was the first job she'd had in a long time where they seemed to expect her to have a brain and to use it.

David stood outside his office building, waiting. It was a smallish building, Tony noted, housing both Tachyon and a travel agency. Still, it was David's own office, and it sounded like Tachyon was well on its way to an impressive expansion.

David greeted her with a bright smile. He wore a collared shirt, a sports coat and khakis, and a tie covered with tiny pink pigs. It must be nice to be able to dress so casually at work, Tony thought, feeling her camisole slipping down for the zillionth time that day. Then again, he owned the company. He could show up in his underwear if he wanted.

Now *there* was an image she'd have a hard time dispelling. She wondered why her thoughts kept sabotaging her.

"How's the new assignment?" he asked.

He started to walk down the sidewalk, touching her lightly on the back to steer her along with him. It started as a feather-light touch; then his hand flattened a bit, moving down until it shaped the curve of her lower back. Her skin went warm beneath his touch, and the warmth eased down her spine, forward to her belly and lower. She almost shivered. A bit forward of him, she thought, and as he withdrew, she wished he'd do it again.

"It's better than the last one," she said. "Too bad it's only good for two weeks."

"Ever think about looking for something permanent?"

She watched him as he walked next to her. His self-possession impressed her, but it bothered her too. She didn't need another man who would try to overpower her.

"I've thought about it. Temping works out better for me right now, though. It's easier to take time off if I need to."

"How are the classes going?"

"Okay, I guess."

They paused to cross the street; then David gave her an evaluating look. "Do you enjoy school? Is it fun at least?"

"No, it's not." The answer blurted out before Tony could pause to consider. She stopped walking, registering what she'd said. At the same time, she realized the floodgates were coming open again, and she wasn't going to be able to stop herself. He halted next to her, watching as she burst out, "I hate accounting. I wish I never had to take another accounting class in my life."

There. Not much of a flood, but it was the first time she'd admitted this to anyone other than herself. She felt like an anvil had just been removed from her chest. But why now? Why was she able to unload to David?

"Then why take them?" David's question was mild, without accusation.

"Because I need a steady income. Everybody needs accountants. Not very many people need marginally talented artists."

David listened to her calmly, letting her emotions spill over him. He couldn't know how much she needed exactly that—someone who could just listen.

"You're more than marginally talented," he said. "I think you're short-changing yourself."

She didn't quite know how to react to that. It was sweet and complimentary and even supportive. But she couldn't act on any of it. She wasn't even sure she could consider him an unbiased judge of her talent, or lack of same.

Rather than argue, she changed the subject.

"Where are we going?"

"There's a park a few blocks down. I thought we'd pick up subs, then have a picnic. It's a great day for it."

Tony smiled. "That sounds nice."

He shrugged. "I couldn't resist. It's twenty degrees cooler at home. I need the sun."

"Twenty degrees?"

"Okay, maybe fifteen. Disadvantages of altitude, in any case."

Tony needed the sun too. It warmed her face as they resumed walking. David's hand touched hers. She turned to him, smiled and took it. He was pleasant company when he stayed away from the too-probing questions.

Seeming to realize her aversion, David didn't ask her any more questions until they reached Subway, when he asked her what kind of sandwich she wanted. She could forgive him that one. A few minutes later, they stepped back out into the sun.

Something had changed, though. A semi truck had pulled to the side of the road in front of the sub shop, blocking one lane, hazard lights blinking. Fortunately it was a light-traffic street, but a few cars had still backed up behind it.

David frowned and passed the bag of sandwiches to Tony. "I'm going to see if I can help."

"David..." But David had already started toward the truck, though Tony had no idea what he thought he would be able to do. After a moment, she decided the turn of events was more endearing than annoying and started after him.

The truck driver knelt on the ground beside the front set of tires. He apparently had a flat, or perhaps two. David stepped toward him, reaching into an inside pocket of his jacket.

"Excuse me," he said. "Anything I can do to help?" He withdrew a cell phone from his jacket. "I've got a phone—"

The truck driver looked up, and David stopped in his tracks. Tony, a few steps behind, froze. Her hands felt suddenly numb, and she had to look down to be sure she hadn't dropped the bag of sandwiches. Then a pain rose in her chest, and she held very still, afraid that if she moved, she might never breathe again.

"Thanks, buddy," said the driver. "I already called it in, though. Somebody should be by in a half hour or so."

David's hand with the cell phone lowered. Tony couldn't see his face, but his voice thrummed with all the tension of a drawn bowstring.

"Rudy James," he said.

The driver peered at him, squinting against the sun. His unkempt black hair fell forward onto his forehead, not diminishing the impact of his brilliantly blue eyes. He was still thick and broad, none of his muscle gone to fat, none of his looks gone to age.

"Do I know you?" he said.

Tony took a single step back, and finally Rudy saw her. He blinked, then stood slowly, staring.

"Tony?" he said. Tony was pleased to hear her own shock reflected in his voice.

"Rudy," said Tony. "You remember David."

Rudy's head jerked back toward David. "David?"

David tucked the cell phone back into his jacket pocket and put out a hand. "David Peterson."

Rudy blinked, then shook his head in disbelief as he took David's hand. "Good God. I never would have recognized you." His eyes slid to Tony. "You, however, haven't changed a bit."

Yes, I have, dammit. Tony lifted her chin, teeth sliding together, and stepped toward David. She wanted to touch him but didn't want to touch him—wanted Rudy to know she had David's support but didn't want to ask David for that support.

She didn't need to. When she got close enough, David reached out and put an arm around her. Rudy's eyebrows rose, and he looked from one to the other, obviously awaiting an explanation.

When it became apparent he wasn't going to get one, he crossed his arms over his chest and leaned back against the side of the truck. "So, what have you been up to, Peterson?"

David drew Tony a bit closer. Suddenly, Tony didn't feel supported anymore. She felt claimed. She stiffened under David's arm and edged away. He'd defaulted to alpha male—*the woman is mine; back off.* And Tony was defaulting to the place she'd always gone when Rudy pushed too hard—inside herself, behind a brittle shell of resentment and anger that was the only way she'd ever been able to protect herself. If it had been anyone but Rudy challenging David, she might have reacted differently. As it was, every shred of the humiliation she associated with her ex-husband flooded every pore. David didn't seem to notice. Of course he didn't.

Rudy noticed, though. Of course, he had a good deal more experience at flexing his alpha-male muscles. His eyes flicked to her, then back to David. Energy arced between the two men, though Rudy lounged nonchalantly against the truck and David stood loose and unconcerned next to Tony.

"Not much," David said. "Just work."

"You still doing that computer stuff?"

"Oh, yeah. Liked it so much I started my own company."

Rudy gave a slight nod, and his eyes hardened. "Really. How's that going?"

"Not bad." He had drawn Tony even closer, in spite of Tony's silent protest. "We made a tidy profit last year, and we're planning to expand."

Rudy's smile was thin. Tony recognized it—she'd seen it far too often directed at her.

"I'll bet there are plenty of women up in Eagle Creek who'd love to get their hands on your wallet." He slid his gaze toward Tony as David's arm tightened once again around her shoulders.

"Thanks for your concern," David said, "but I can handle things fine."

He started to turn away, drawing Tony with him. Tony held her ground. Her recalcitrance seemed to catch David unaware, and his arm slid away from her shoulders. He turned back toward her, a question on his face.

"So how have you been?" she said to Rudy. In the edge of her vision, she saw David straighten, then shake his head. She turned just as he opened his mouth to speak. She cut him off with a nod. It was okay. She wanted to do this alone. Needed to.

For a moment, she thought he would protest; then he set his lips together and nodded. He turned and continued down the sidewalk.

Tony turned back to see Rudy watching David's departing figure. She bit the inside of her lower lip, unsure what else to do, or say. She didn't want to talk to Rudy—up until five minutes ago, she would have said that if she ever saw Rudy again, she would either run the other way or commit violence on his person. Yet here she was trying to come up with small talk, and for what reason? She wasn't sure, but with David's possessive arm gone from around her, she felt steadier.

She started to step away, to pretend she hadn't asked Rudy anything at all. Then he turned back toward her, and his eyes held her.

"I'm okay, Tony. How about you?"

She remembered, then, why she'd stayed with him so long. Because when he'd been on the road, she hadn't remembered the way he'd controlled her, the way he had of knocking her down the moment she found steadiness beneath her feet. All she had ever remembered was that square jaw and those blue, blue eyes.

And what did she have now? She could face this down—she knew she could. Suddenly, David's presence felt more protective than possessive, his withdrawal at her silent request not abandonment but trust in her strength.

"I'm great," she said. She started to say more, to explain exactly how great, but in a flash of insight, she realized he'd never understand, and that nothing would ever make him see her any differently. And she didn't care. She didn't need his presence or his approval. She was strong, dammit. He couldn't take that away from her.

Rudy nodded. "That's good." His face was expressionless, and she could read nothing in his eyes. It had always been that way with him. He'd closed himself off, kept his face and his eyes empty. She'd never really understood why. She'd never really understood anything about him.

His gaze moved down a bit, as if he was looking at her mouth, then he looked back up again. "Are you happy with him?"

Tony gave an exasperated sigh. "I'm not..." She stopped. He didn't get explanations. He didn't deserve them. She closed her eyes a moment to break the blue spell of his eyes. "Look, Rudy, I have to get going. It was good seeing you."

She took a step back and started to turn.

"Hey, Tony."

His voice stopped her; she wasn't sure why. She looked at him with her head tilted, her mouth tight and her back stiff.

"Give me a call sometime," he said.

To her own surprise, she smiled. "Yeah, maybe I will." She took another step back. "If you—if you need the phone, we'll be a block or so down the road at the park."

And finally she turned completely and moved away, and something inside her that had been tight and hurtful opened up, seeming to loosen more with each step she took away from him.

David had stopped a short distance away, far enough he wouldn't have been able to hear anything either of them had said but close enough he could have watched the exchange. He took a step toward her as she approached, an expression of concern on his face.

"Are you all right?"

Tony nodded. "I'm fine."

"What did he say to you?"

"Nothing. Just... I can't—" She'd been strong. She'd faced the dragon. Now she wanted to crawl into a hole and cry like crying was going out of style. She brushed past him, continuing down the sidewalk. She didn't want him to see her like this. She just wanted to do it on her own.

"Tony! Tony, wait up."

She didn't wait up, but he caught her and took her arm, slowing her down. "Tony, are you okay?"

"No. Yes..." She pulled her arm free of his grasp. His touch made all the emotions roil again, and she was trying to get them under control. "Let's just go on to the park. Maybe I'll feel better once I get something to eat."

David said nothing until they arrived at the little park. They sat down on a bench. Tony found herself relaxing somewhat as she watched a woman tail two small boys through the play area. She caught one, tucked him under her arm, then grabbed the other's hand and they ran, laughing, toward the jungle gym.

After a moment, she realized she was smiling. David must have noticed, for just then he said, "Could I have my sandwich now?"

It was enough to break a good bit of the tension. Tony laughed and gave him the bag. She'd completely forgotten she still had his sandwich. He pulled it out, then passed the bag back. He unwrapped the sub and took a bite, studying her while he chewed.

"I'm sorry," he said finally. "That whole thing just caught me by surprise. I should have backed off earlier, let you handle it."

Dealing with David

Tony snorted. "Caught *you* by surprise? I tossed the man out on his ass and I haven't laid an eye on him in three years, and all of a sudden he shows up by the side of the road? That's more than just a surprise. That's enough to give a person a coronary."

David chuckled and shook his head. "Yeah, and—"

"Three years. Three *years*. And he shows up out of nowhere? And then you got all weird. I swear, the alpha-dog thing just isn't attractive on anybody—"

"I said I was sorry—"

"My God, what did he think? He could just cruise back into town and throw me over his shoulder and drag me off to his cave?"

"Tony—"

"I mean, what the hell? Seriously. What. The. *Hell?*" She was fuming now, all the adrenaline the encounter had engendered draining out of her in the pointless rant. "And what were you doing? I'm not your property, you know."

"I know. I just—"

"He doesn't own me. He never did. Nobody does, dammit." Where the hell was this going? She couldn't stop. It was as if someone had flipped a switch, and she couldn't find the off button. "I can't believe he just—"

"Tony!"

Tony's mouth snapped shut, and she stared at David. In spite of the strength of his sudden bellow, he was smiling.

"Tony," he repeated more quietly, "you're dropping your tomatoes."

Tony looked at her sandwich and, sheepish, gathered the wayward pieces back together. For good measure, she took a bite. Maybe shoving food in her mouth would shut off the torrent.

"I said I was sorry," David said as she chewed. "And I really wasn't staking a claim. Seriously, I'm not an alpha dog. I'm like—I don't know—one of those pit bulls on YouTube that plays with baby ducks. I just..." He broke off as Tony gave him a skeptically quirked brow. "He hurt you once. I couldn't just stand there and watch him do it again."

That brought Tony up short. Mentally, she chewed on that as thoroughly as she chewed on her bite of sandwich. He claimed protectiveness, not possession. After a moment, she shook her head.

"I can take care of myself, David. I don't need you to protect me."

"I know." He readjusted the paper wrapping on his sandwich. "I'm sorry it seemed that way to you. It wasn't what I intended."

Silence reigned for a minute or so while they ate. David seemed to realize Tony needed more time to cool down. Her heart rate had finally returned to normal, and eating the sandwich was gradually dampening the post-adrenaline queasiness.

Tony's anger continued to diffuse the more she thought about what David had said. She didn't like being dependent, she didn't like being treated like a possession, but she rather liked the idea of having someone who felt the need to protect her. Not that she needed protection, of course. But it was a nice feeling.

"Okay, I forgive you," she said finally. She wadded up her sandwich's paper wrapper and put it back in the bag. "And I'm sorry I overreacted."

David nodded. "It's okay. You're allowed to overreact, given the situation." He wadded up his own sandwich wrapper and gave her a mock-chastising look. "Just don't let it happen again."

Tony laughed, then leaned back on the park bench, letting the warm sun caress her face. It felt good to know she had just walked away from Rudy. And it was the last time, she decided. She wasn't going to call him. She had no reason to. "You asked what he said to me?"

"Yeah." David's tone was wary.

Tony grinned. "I kinda kicked his ass."

David laughed. "Good for you." He paused. "If you hadn't, I would have. Literally."

She nodded. "I might have to think that over for a while to decide if that's okay with me."

"Fair enough."

They were quiet again for a time, then another thought crossed her mind, dark and unwelcome. She straightened again and looked at David.

"You didn't believe him. I mean, what he said about me wanting into your wallet."

To Tony's surprise, David reached over and slipped his hand under hers. His long fingers wove through hers. "I don't. If you did, you'd be working harder at it."

She laughed. Her gaze fixed on his full lower lip, remembering the way his mouth had felt on hers.

"Maybe it's selfish of me," he said quietly, "but I'm glad he saw you happy. And I'm glad you were with me when it happened." Shifting, he turned to face her more fully. "It's all I want for you. Really. To be happy. And if I keep bringing up your art, that's why. I think it's what would make you happy.

Sometimes you have to take those risks. I learned that when I took the leap to work with Rich and put Tachyon together." His hand tightened on hers a little. "You're that talented, Tony. You really are."

Her heart moved within her, as if trying to spread long-folded wings. Then she heard her mother's voice telling her not to waste her time doodling when she should be doing something useful. She heard Rudy telling her she should have known her designs wouldn't sell, and now could she please act like a normal person again?

David's hand moved on hers. The touch was warm and real, and at the moment it felt like a lifeline.

"You said you tried art before. What happened?"

Tony swallowed. She owed him an explanation, she supposed, after all the times she'd steered him away from the topic. "It was just a stupid idea I had for a business. It didn't fly."

"Tell me."

"No, it's just embarrassing now."

"Why? What did you do? Specialize in decorative tattoos for unmentionable portions of the male anatomy?"

Tony smiled. Maybe this was why she kept spilling her guts—because he made it so easy. "No. I painted shirts. T-shirts, denim shirts—you know. I did custom designs, Western designs, Egyptian hieroglyphics." Some of the old excitement crept into her voice. Hearing it, she quelled it. She tried to pull her hand away from David's, but he moved just enough to make it difficult for her to free herself. "Well," Tony went on. "It seemed like a good idea at the time."

"It still sounds like a good idea. Where did you sell them?"

"I *tried* to sell them at flea markets here and there, and online. It didn't go well, so I quit."

"How long did you work at it?"

"Six months."

David shrugged. "There you go. You quit too soon."

Tony considered saying nothing, since he seemed not to require an answer. But she couldn't fight an urge to defend herself.

"It was all the time Rudy would give me."

David nodded slowly. Something moved in his eyes, some powerful emotion that made Tony weak with desire.

"I'll give you all the time you need."

Tony's hand tightened involuntarily on his, feeling the strength of his bones, the lines of his long, warm fingers. He returned her grasp just as strongly, then released her.

"Let's walk," he said.

They strolled the rest of the way around the block, taking the long way back to David's office. Tony knew it was to avoid passing by Rudy again, but she enjoyed the chance to stretch her legs and enjoy the sun.

About halfway around the block, David's hand caught hers, and she let him draw her closer. When they stopped in front of his building, he turned and took her other hand, holding her out in front of him.

He looked at her a moment, then said, "How'd you like to go sledding Saturday?"

Tony laughed. "Sledding?" She could just picture the two of them careening down some snow-packed hill like a couple of goofy kids.

David grinned. "Sure. C'mon, it's Colorado for Pete's sake. And the best sledding hill in Eagle Creek still has about six inches of snow on it 'cause it's in the shade."

Tony looked at him, shaking her head. How could she turn him down? "Sure. Why not?"

"Great. Do you remember how to get to my house?"

"More or less."

She gave him a piece of paper from her purse, and he jotted down directions to refresh her memory, adding the street address in case her GPS could actually navigate the high mountain neighborhoods. "I'll see you Saturday, then. Two okay?"

"That's fine."

He stood on the sidewalk and watched while she went back to her car. In turn, she watched him walk up the stairs and into the building, mesmerized by the soft swing of his jacket and the rhythm of his lanky walk.

There was no point fighting it anymore. The pull toward him had gotten too strong. She wasn't sure yet if it was love, but she'd reached the crossroads where she could either follow that path or run the other way.

She turned the key in the ignition. For the moment, she would follow it.

Chapter Eight

David put in a few hours of work Saturday morning, still hammering out problems with *Dark Princes III*. Somewhere between ten and ten thirty, he finally pieced together a logical series of events to bring Aethelfried through the last stages of action in the Black Castle.

That left him mentally exhausted, so he booted up *Dark Princes II* and slaughtered orcs until lunchtime.

Two bologna sandwiches and a Coors later, he was reduced to the mood of a teenager waiting for a prom date. Surfing through channels on the TV, he barely registered what he was watching.

His thoughts overflowed with Tony. He wondered what color her eyes would be today—her brand of hazel seemed to shift with her mood. How would she do her hair? Would it be up or loose, so he could run his fingers through it?

It was time to test her again, he thought, see how far she'd let him go. God, he wanted her so much it was starting to physically hurt, almost like he had the flu. Was this what the term lovesick meant?

Her car found his driveway at one thirty. A few minutes later, he answered her knock, and his questions were answered.

Her eyes were as green as he'd ever seen them, her dark blonde hair drawn back into a ponytail. Before he could think about it, he bent forward and kissed her cheek. The soft skin beneath his lips only reminded him what it had been like to feel her mouth open under his. He ached with wanting her, in his heart and other parts.

"Sorry I'm so early," she said as he stepped back. She walked around him without touching him, almost as if she were avoiding contact. "I wasn't sure how long it would take, since I was driving in snow last time."

"No problem. Our hill reservations aren't until two, but I think they might let us in early." Her absent smile at the lame joke wasn't quite what he'd been after. He stepped back from the doorway. "Come on in. I just have to grab a couple of things."

He pulled his coat from the closet and led the way downstairs. He had already tossed a pair of lightweight plastic sleds into the back of the Jeep, so they were underway in a matter of minutes.

Shadow Hill crawled with kids, from toddlers building snowmen with their parents to teenagers manufacturing moguls which they plowed over at breakneck speed on inner tubes or plastic sleds. The slopes lay in a mountainous shadow, and an insistent, chilly breeze swept the hillside. A few hundred feet away, where the shadow ended, the snow was gone, the slopes decorated instead with brown grass and patches of mud. Tony pulled gloves and earmuffs from her coat pockets and put them on while David retrieved the sleds.

"I didn't think it'd be this cold," Tony said. She stiffened her arms and jumped up and down a few times. She looked adorable in her bright pink earmuffs.

David smiled, looking at her. He couldn't help it. He might as well give up and admit it. He was achingly, helplessly in love with her, every bit as much as he had been the day he'd first laid eyes on her. Some things just didn't change with maturity. They aged, like wine, becoming sweeter and more complexly flavored. It took nothing to make his body respond to her, and now he couldn't blame it on rampant adolescent hormones. She adjusted her earmuffs, and he hurt, more than just with physical desire—all the way to his soul.

"It's always cold here," he reminded her. "That's why it's such a good place for sledding."

He tucked the sleds under his arm and reached for her gloved hand with his own. She smiled at him as she took it.

They trudged up the steep, slippery hill. David tried to steer them onto virgin snow, where the footing would be better, but after two weeks of prime sledding conditions, there was very little of it left. Tony slipped, and David tightened his grip on her hand, keeping her upright. A few steps later, David's feet tried to go out from under him, and Tony clutched his arm, supporting his weight for the second or two it took him to steady himself. They both ended up laughing.

She looked happy. It had saddened him on their last date to see the old pain in her eyes. Rudy had had a wonderful thing and had done his best to ruin it. David still wished he'd taken the chance to pop Rudy a good one. Not that it would have done any good. With his luck, he would have ended up in jail, and Tony certainly wouldn't have appreciated the show of alpha male-ness. But, facing Rudy in those moments, he'd felt like the pit bull that was done playing with the baby ducks and was ready to protect its family from knife-wielding intruders. Maybe he had an alpha streak after all. Just a little one. Teeny tiny.

Well, David, unlike Rudy, knew a good thing when he saw it. He wanted nothing more than to see Tony happy. If he had his way about it, he'd be sure she stayed happy for the rest of her life. The realization surprised him. He wasn't sure why. His brain and his heart had both been heading that way for a while now—one of the few times they'd ever been in complete accord. He wanted to give her everything.

Briefly, he wondered if he should mention the pictures. Rich wouldn't show them to the design team until Monday, though, so he decided against it. There was no point getting Tony's hopes up. His own hopes were already up for both of them.

A line of teenagers had formed at the top of the hill, waiting to descend the roughest stretch. A complex series of snow ramps and hills marked the trail.

"Looks like fun," Tony said. She looked a bit worried, though, as if she were hesitant to stand in line with a bunch of teenage boys, with their tendencies toward obnoxious rowdiness.

David had no such compunctions. Teenage boys, after all, had spent a good bit of their hard-earned allowances to bring home *Dark Princes*.

"Let's go," he said and tugged Tony after him.

The two young men in front of them were involved in an animated conversation. David couldn't help overhearing.

"I got as far as the Troll Bridge, but I can't answer the riddles." The boy shook his head. "I gotta get past this. *Dark Princes II* comes out next week, and Mom won't let me buy it until I finish the first one."

The other boy seemed sympathetic but couldn't offer much help. "Man, I remember the bridge, but I don't remember the answers to the riddles."

David grinned. Moments like these were rare, and he loved them. It was one thing to see the sales reports and know that *Dark Princes* sold so fast stores could barely keep it on the shelves, but it was quite another to see firsthand evidence of the game's popularity. He cleared his throat into a gloved fist.

"There are clues on the screen," he said. The boys turned, apparently not entirely sure he was speaking to them. "If you click on the shrubbery, it'll talk to you and help you out."

"No way!" The boy who had finished the game had obviously done so without aid from online vegetation.

The other boy seemed equally impressed. "You played *Dark Princes*? Did you finish it?"

"I played it about a thousand times," David said, still grinning. "I wrote it." He stuck out his free hand, the one that wasn't attached to Tony. "David Peterson, Tachyon Software."

"No *way*!" The first boy took a step backward. "I was on an online conference you did last month about *Dark Princes II*. Is there really going to be another one?"

"Absolutely. *Dark Princes III* should be out early next year."

He glanced at Tony. Her warm smile made him tingle.

"This your wife?" the older boy said.

David squeezed Tony's hand. "Afraid not."

"Girlfriend?"

"Working on it." He carefully avoided looking at Tony, afraid her reaction to his statement would be less than positive.

They'd reached the head of the line by then. The two boys were sharing a toboggan. As they positioned themselves, the older boy gave him a thumbs-up.

"Good luck, Mr. Peterson!"

David handed Tony her sled as the boys disappeared, whooping their appreciation of the enhanced slopes.

"Working on it?" Tony repeated with a disapproving look. Her eyes were smiling, though. Good. She'd taken the comment in the right spirit.

David shrugged. "I make it a habit not to lie to children."

Tony poked him playfully in the back. "Get going. It's your turn."

David flopped onto the plastic sled and went howling down the hill.

Tony couldn't remember the last time she'd had so much fun. After three trips down the slope, she started following David more closely, thinking she might be able to catch him partway down. When she tried to speed up, though, she wiped out on the second hill and slid the rest of the way down headfirst on her belly.

David met her at the bottom of the hill.

"You okay?" he asked, kneeling next to her.

Tony burst out laughing. Her nose was running, and she couldn't feel her earlobes, in spite of the earmuffs. David grinned back at her and held out his hand. She took it, letting him pull her to her feet.

"I'm fine," she said. Her yellow plastic sled joined her at the bottom of the hill. David bent and picked it up, tucked both sleds under one arm and Tony under the other.

"Let's go down together," he said.

Tony wondered momentarily if he'd lost his mind. "What?"

"You. Me. Sled. Downhill." He made a sweeping gesture with his hand to clarify, as if Tony might not be able to follow his monosyllables.

"There's not enough room on that sled for both of us!" She slogged back up the hill after him, feet sliding in the hard-packed snow.

"Sure there is." He reached back and caught her hand, helping her up the slope.

"But with so much weight, won't we go too fast?"

"Speak for yourself." David's grin had become pure evil. "I'm quite svelte."

Tony was left with little option but to laugh and follow him back to the top of the hill.

The two *Dark Princes* players—Matt and Brian—met them again in the line. They'd been crisscrossing paths fairly consistently since their initial meeting, though the boys had taken a break from this run to try a slightly fresher—and steeper—slope a few yards down the hill.

"It's getting icy down there," Matt said. Tony noticed he was limping.

"Are you all right?"

Matt shrugged, grinning the way teenage boys do when they're awed by pretty women but don't want to admit it. "Just twisted my ankle trying to get stopped." His expression went suddenly serious. Tony couldn't help but be flattered by the obvious effect she had on him. "You be careful down there. I don't want anybody getting busted up on my shift."

David laughed and wrapped a protective arm around Tony's shoulders. "Don't worry. I'll take care of her."

At the top of the hill, David stacked the two plastic toboggans, one inside the other.

"That'll hold us fine," he said to Tony. "Are you game?"

Tony shrugged. She was fully into the spirit of the venture now and had to admit the prospect of sharing a kids' plastic sled with David held a great deal of appeal. "Sure, why not?"

"Just watch the last five yards or so," Brian cautioned. They'd acquired a second sled, and Matt had already plummeted down, whooping enthusiastically. "Steer to the left if you can. That'll keep you off the icy patch. Going down by yourself you won't have hit that spot, but with both of you on board you're pretty much guaranteed to."

He readied his own sled then, as Matt wiped out at the base of the hill.

"Thanks for the tip," David said. Brian was off with a respectable wail. David set the combined sleds on the ground and flopped into them, digging a heel into the snow to keep stationary while Tony joined him.

The small sled made a tight but pleasant fit. Tony sat securely tucked between David's long legs, her back against his chest. He put his arms around her and set his mouth against her ear.

"If we come out of this alive," he whispered, "you have to promise to kiss me."

Tony barely registered his words. His breath against the back of her ear warmed her more than her heavy parka ever could. At this rate, he could ask for a good deal more than a kiss.

"Okay, I promise," she said.

David seemed surprised. "Really? I thought you wanted to keep this social."

"I..."Ahead of them, Brian had hit the bottom of the slope and was rolling out of his sled. "It's our turn. We can talk about this later."

David maneuvered their sled to the starting position and waited until Brian was completely in the clear. Then he tucked Tony's head under his chin, and with a good, solid kick, they were off.

At first, the increased weight on the sled bogged them down. Then they reached the first steep drop, and Tony immediately felt the difference in their speed. The chilly wind whipped her face, bringing wind-tears to her eyes. She sank farther back against David's chest, hanging on to the edge of the sled for all she was worth.

She knew the first constructed hill was coming, but still it caught her by surprise when she saw the ridge of hard-packed snow and felt the front of the sled rise sharply under her. Then they were in the air. Behind her, David whooped his enthusiasm. The shout would have been loud enough to hurt her ear if the wind hadn't grabbed it and flung it away.

They landed hard—and wrong. The sled continued at its pell-mell pace, traveling sideways.

"This is not good!" David shouted.

Tony felt him shift behind her; then he put a foot out into the snow, trying to steer. His boot skidded across the hard-packed, icy surface, and the sled turned more sideways.

Tony put her foot out on the other side, hoping to compensate for David's failure. It proved a bad move. The snow didn't yield to her foot any better than it had to David's. And before she could draw her foot back in, they had reached the second hill. Sliding sideways.

She tried to get back in the sled, but something trapped her foot against the sled. Pain shot hot up her leg, then the sled flipped over the top of the snow ramp and she was airborne.

She seemed to be in the air forever, but it couldn't have been more than a half second. Then she came back down.

She landed hard, on her back, in the icy hard snow. Stars filled her vision as the impact knocked her breath away. In the temporary haze she felt herself sliding, sliding, then rolling, the snow buffeting and bruising her, until she finally stopped at the foot of the hill.

David skidded to a stop and looked up, searching for Tony. He had managed to stay in the sled, but she had been flung free.

Normally he wouldn't have worried. She couldn't have gone too far, and even if she'd slid to the bottom of the hill, there weren't any trees or similar dangers, nor could she have slid into the road. But he'd heard her cry of pain just before the jolt of the second jump had flung her free. He searched and saw her, came to his feet and ran, unmindful of the slippery snow beneath his feet.

She lay spread-eagled at the base of the hill, still, staring straight up at the bright blue sky. Even from this distance he could tell her face was far too pale. As he ran toward her, she moved, trying to get up, then fell back with a grimace of pain.

It seemed an eternity before he skidded to a stop beside her, falling to his knees. She had managed to turn onto one side, but her face was still tight and pale.

"Tony, are you all right?" God, she'd broken her leg or hurt her back, all because of his stupid daredevil sled tricks.

"My ankle," Tony said, her voice thin. "I twisted it, I think."

David put his hands around the ankle in question, carefully trying to rotate it. Vaguely he noticed Matt and Brian running toward them.

"I don't think it's broken," David said, relieved. "You probably just gave it a good wrench."

The boys had stopped. "Is she okay, Mr. Peterson?" Matt asked. "Should we call 911?"

"No," said Tony. "I don't think that's necessary."

She started to get up, but David stopped her with a hand on her shoulder. He didn't want her trying to move anymore until he was sure she wasn't badly hurt.

"Did you hurt anything else?" he said.

Tony hesitated, moving her head from side to side as if testing her neck. "No, I don't think so. Just a few scrapes and bruises."

"All right." David decided to accept her diagnosis. "Can you stand up?"

As carefully as he could, he lifted Tony to her feet, easing her weight over onto himself as he did so. She leaned against him, standing steadily on one foot, but when she gingerly touched the other foot to the ground she winced and sucked in a sharp breath.

"It's bad?" David said.

Tony nodded, wordless, face white. David swallowed his anxiety. Just a wrench, he thought, surely just a wrench, but how could he have been so stupid? How could he have endangered her? He carefully bent and picked her up, cradling her sweet, slight body against his chest.

"Is there anything we can do?" This was Brian's voice, at his elbow.

"Could you grab the sleds? That'd be a big help."

The boys retrieved the plastic sleds and trailed after David as he carried Tony back to the Jeep. She was still and quiet against him. Her silence tore his heart out. He glanced at her face and saw closed lids, tears beading them. He was afraid even to ask her again if she was all right.

At the car, David turned to Matt.

"My car keys are in my right coat pocket." Matt retrieved the keys and opened the Jeep. David set Tony carefully inside.

"Stay put," he told her. "I have to put the sleds in the back." He paused, studying her face. She had opened her eyes, and they still glistened, but no tears had fallen. Her arms were folded across her chest, and she looked miserable. David didn't know what to say, so he said nothing.

The boys loaded the sleds into the back; then David closed and locked the hatch.

"Don't go yet," he told the boys. He reached into the Jeep, across Tony, into the glove compartment to pull out a notepad and a pen. Hastily, he scribbled notes on the first two sheets.

"Take these to the office in Lakewood," he said. "I've written the address down. Give the receptionist this note, and she'll take care of you."

The boys read the notes, eyes widening.

"Is this for real?" Matt said. "They'll really give us free copies of *Dark Princes II*?"

"Absolutely." He closed the door to the Jeep, giving Tony another concerned look. Her face had softened, but she still looked pained. "Take it easy out there," he told the boys as he crossed to the driver's side. "Thanks for your help."

He closed the driver's side door, gave Tony one last, long look, and started the car.

Chapter Nine

Tony hunched in the passenger seat of the Jeep, waiting for the other shoe to drop. The pain in her ankle had subsided a bit, but it still throbbed unbearably. She watched David, wary, as he got in the car and started the ignition.

"Are you sure you're okay?" he asked. "There's a doctor's office right on Eagle Street."

"I don't need to see a doctor." Her voice shook in spite of her efforts to keep it steady. "They're probably not open on Saturday, anyway."

"That's probably true." He shifted his grip on the steering wheel, his knuckles going white.

Suddenly, David exploded, slamming his fist into the steering wheel. "Dammit!"

Tony flinched, sinking into the seat. "I'm sorry," she said, barely able to do more than mouth the words.

"*You're* sorry?" David was angry. Fuming. Tony didn't blame him. She'd been an idiot to stick her foot out of the sled like that. She deserved a sprained ankle.

But David wasn't finished. "*You're* sorry? Why the hell should *you* be sorry? It was my stupid idea to go down together."

Tony blinked. "It was just an accident. It wasn't your fault." Then she stopped, chewed on her lips. "You're not mad at me?"

"No. Why would I be mad at you?"

Tony didn't supply the answer. Rudy would have been furious, demanding to know why she was so stupid. She thought she'd finally left the last of Rudy's baggage behind, but she couldn't shake the picture of his anger as it had been directed toward her so many times.

After a time, during which she tried to bring her reactions back around to reality, she said, "There's no point blaming yourself, either."

They turned onto David's street, winding their way up the mountain.

"It was a stupid idea. I should have known better. We should have done something adults do, instead of running around acting like kids."

"But it was fun," Tony protested. David swung his head around, surprised. "I mean, up until the dire-injury phase."

He grinned finally, a not-quite-humorous twist of his mouth. "You should know better than to listen to me."

The pain seemed to have subsided a bit by the time they pulled into David's garage. Tony was able to hobble with some support into the house but balked when she got to the stairs. David carried her up and set her on the couch, then went into the kitchen.

While David gathered ice cubes and put them in a Ziploc bag, Tony carefully unlaced her boots and pulled them off. Her ankle had swollen visibly and was turning very interesting colors seemingly before her eyes. Coming back with the ice pack and a bottle of ibuprofen, David gave a low whistle.

His face creased into a deep frown as he knelt in front of her. Gently, he applied the bag of ice, holding it carefully against the bruises. Tony flinched at the cold, then forced herself to hold her leg steady.

"Mom always said frozen peas were best for this kind of thing."

Tony looked at him dubiously, wondering if he'd hit his head in the tumble down the hill. "Frozen peas?"

"Yeah. A bag of peas makes a good ice pack because you can shape it around the injury." He looked morose. "I'm afraid I don't have any, though. I never was much for peas."

Tony couldn't help smiling. "It's okay, David." He looked up at her from where he sat crouched on the floor in front of her. She reached toward him, sliding her hand along his cheek. He looked like he hadn't shaved this morning, and the faint bristle of his beard tickled her palm.

"I'll be okay," she said. "It's just a sprain. It feels better already."

He smiled ruefully, then grinned, shaking his head.

"What?"

"I was just trying to figure out how I could kiss you without letting go of this ice pack."

The pain seemed to disappear. All she could feel was the sudden strength of his caring, the unexpected depths of her own. She leaned toward him, cupping her hand behind his head. Her fingers burrowed through his thick, dark hair, finding the warmth of his scalp. His gray eyes seemed darker, a winter storm color. Tony felt weak.

His hand on the ice pack shifted as she fitted her lips to his, but he kept the cold where it needed to be. Tony leaned into him, carried on her own surge of passion, pressing his mouth open with her own. A rapid, melting sense of need washed down her, pooling in her belly and below.

He made a small sound of surprise as he welcomed her advance. His tongue found hers in a soft caress. His free hand touched her face, her throat, her collar, then slid down to cup her breast. His thumb flicked her nipple, and a sharp pulse of feeling arrowed straight through her. She'd never felt quite this way before. Involuntarily, she leaned farther into him, taking everything he had to give her, giving everything she had to give.

David broke away first, leaning back to look at her with a dark smolder in his eyes. Tony bit her lip. That look in his eyes filled her up with heat. She knew exactly what he wanted. She wanted it too.

But instead of trying to claim it, David rocked back a bit farther. He looked at her ankle to be sure the ice pack was still in place.

"Let me get you something to drink so you can take some ibuprofen," he said without looking at her. "What would you like?"

Tony swallowed. Why was he backing away? Had she done something wrong?

"Hot chocolate?" She could barely get the words out.

He nodded and pushed himself to his feet. The movement pulled his jeans tight, and Tony saw that their kiss had affected him much as it had her. On a physical level, anyway. She could only guess at his emotions.

When he came back with the mug of hot chocolate, he sat on the couch next to her. Tony had rearranged her feet so the ice pack was secured between her ankles. She deliberately touched David's fingers as she took the mug, feeling the warmth of his skin against hers.

"TV?" he said.

Tony nodded. The hot chocolate tasted bitter in her mouth. Schooling her features, she swallowed it.

David, picking up the remote control as he sipped from his own steaming mug, had no such compunction. He made a face, stopping just short of spitting the cocoa back into the cup.

"God, this is awful. I forgot the sugar." He retrieved Tony's cup and went back into the kitchen. When he returned, he sat down next to her again, but a few inches farther away.

Tony tasted the cocoa again. It was fine now—slightly too sweet, in fact.

David, on the other hand, was *not* fine. He was acting quite strange. He turned on the TV and began to flip channels. Looking at his eyes, Tony could tell he wasn't even registering what was on the screen.

She took another long drink of cocoa to steady herself.

"David?"

He glanced at her, a quick flit of his eyes, then turned back to the TV. "What?"

"What's wrong?"

"Nothing," he said, too quickly. "Nothing's wrong. I'm fine."

Tony blinked hard a few times and took another drink. The cocoa sat warm and rich in her stomach.

"David... Are you mad at me?"

This time he turned and looked straight at her, frowning with perplexity. "No. Why in the world would I be mad at you?"

"Because—" *Because Rudy would have been.* "Because I was stupid enough to stick my foot out and get it almost twisted off."

David shook his head slowly. His expression was unreadable. Tony tried to pick the threads of emotion out of it. Anger, for certain, even if not directed at her. Confusion, surprise, and something else, something so soft and yet so profound that she turned suddenly away, afraid she hadn't seen it.

"No, I'm not mad at you," David said again. "I'm mad at myself because it was my dumb idea to go down together, and because..." He stopped and stared again at the TV, apparently unaware he had stopped on a station broadcasting nothing but snow.

"Because?" Tony prompted.

He shook his head sharply and stood. "Nothing. How's the ankle?"

Tony wanted very much to know what he had been about to say but decided to let it drop. She shifted her feet, letting the ice pack fall away from her injured ankle. The swelling seemed to have decreased some. Her skin was numb from the ice.

"It looks better." She bent to move the ice pack. "Frankly, I don't think I can stand this ice pack much longer."

"We might as well wrap it up, then." He started down the hallway. "I think I've got an Ace bandage around here somewhere."

Tony finished her cocoa and took her pills while David rooted noisily somewhere in the back of the house. She couldn't tell if he was trying to withdraw emotionally because she was hurt, or because he'd decided to back off to give her space, or because he'd just plain changed his mind. She did know one thing, though—she wanted to feel his hand on her breast again. Wanted to feel his mouth there. She wanted to know what the skin on the insides of his thighs felt like, if it was soft and hairless for just an inch or so before rising to his groin...

He returned with the bandage and knelt in front of her, gently lifting her bare foot. His big, graceful hands cradled her heel, then carefully began to wrap the bandage.

The pain had diminished considerably since the initial shock of the injury, but the joint still twinged a bit, even as careful as he was, as he neatly bound foot and ankle in swaths of tan cloth. The bandage had a faint, medicinal odor, as if it had been used before with Bengay or something. Tony looked down at his softly moving hands and knew that, now and forever, she would associate that smell with things erotic. That was going to be super weird in her old age, she was certain.

The touch of his hands charged her skin, sending tendrils of sensation curling up under her calf to settle in the soft place behind her knee. If only he would move his hands higher, and touch her there...

He sat back on his heels, eyeing his handiwork with a deep, almost foreboding frown.

"That'll do," he said. He started to look up at her, then turned his attention back to her leg instead. "You should undo it later, probably before bed, and soak it or put another ice pack on it."

"Thank you," she said.

He spared her a glance, then stood, picked up her empty mug and headed for the kitchen.

Tony watched him, her mouth thinning, and made a decision. She got up and hobbled to the closet for her coat.

"What are you doing?" David stopped short just inside the kitchen door, looking at her like she'd slapped him.

"I'm leaving," she said. Much to her surprise, her voice cracked. Coat over her arm, she hobbled back to the couch to struggle with her boots. Tears burned in her eyes and she blinked them back, swallowing to repair her voice. "I'm going home."

"Tony, don't be silly—"

"Now I'm silly." Anger took over from the emptiness which had settled in her stomach. Good. Anger was much easier to deal with. "I knew it was something like that. I was just too dumb to get down the hill without half killing myself, and now you're trying to come up with a polite way to ask me to leave—"

"Tony, stop. Please."

The forceful tone brought her up short. David was glaring at her, blazing in absolute fury. Tony folded her hands in her lap and tried to make herself very small. Rudy had never hit her, but he'd come close, and both times he'd had nearly that same look in his eyes. David stayed where he was, though, hands loose and open.

"Will you listen to me for two seconds, please? How many times do I have to tell you I'm *not* angry with you?" He broke off, and his fury eased a bit as some point of irony hit home. "Well, okay, yes, I'm angry at you, but not because you fell out of the sled. That would be stupid."

"Then why?"

"Because you're putting your coat on." His voice had quieted to a normal volume, and the anger seemed to slide off him. "Because every time we get—close—the next thing I know, you're walking away from me."

Tony had managed to work her sock back on, but the effort left her biting her lip in pain.

"Look what you're doing to yourself," David said, gesturing toward her foot. "Do you really want to get away from me so badly you're willing to drive in that condition?"

Anger came in a hard, sharp wave and seemed to fill Tony's head. "Do I repulse you so much that you have to jump up and make hot chocolate every ten seconds or turn on the TV and watch nothing?" She shot to her feet, the dramatic effect somewhat hampered by her need to grab the back of the couch to keep from falling on her face. "I'm not good enough for you, am I? Is that what it is? It was fine to be all goggly about me when you were just nerdy David Peterson, but now that you're Mr. Tachyon Software, a struggling, badly educated divorcée is just way too below your level. Right?"

She was screaming at him, tears flying, appalled at her own words. She wanted to hit him. She wanted to tear his clothes off and make love to him until they both died of heart failure. She wanted to turn around, get in her car and leave, and never lay eyes on him again.

David just stood there, gaping at her, an expression of complete befuddlement driving the anger from his face.

"Is that what you think?" His voice had lowered, the anger changing to hurt. Tony crossed her arms over her chest, holding her shoulders, trying to slow her rapid breathing, to bring her raging emotions back under control. She couldn't find an answer inside the maelstrom—couldn't find anything coherent at all.

After a long moment, David took a step forward.

"Sit back down," he said. "Sit down and let me talk for a minute."

Tony sank onto the couch, relieved to take her weight off her throbbing ankle. David walked around the couch and sat down next to her. This time he sat close and lifted both her hands in his.

"You need to understand something, Tony." She shifted uncomfortably in his grasp, unsure what he was going to say but sure somehow that it would change everything. "I was in love with you in high school, and I'm just as in love with you now. More so, even. You are beautiful and brave, and I admire what you've done with your life. My only regret is that you had to spend so long with that idiot Rudy. Because if this is what he did to you, he doesn't deserve you or any other woman."

"You're"—she wasn't sure she could get the words out—"in love with me?"

He nodded. "And the reason I kept getting up to make hot chocolate or whatever is that I can't even give you first aid without wanting to—" He broke off, clearly grasping for words. Finally he said, with a wry grin, "To ravish you shamelessly, as Aethelfried might say. And you're hurt. I can't—"

"Yes, you can."

He swallowed. Tony could hear it, could see the strangely slow downward movement of his Adam's apple. That dark, winter-storm look came into his eyes again. "I can—what?"

Tony felt herself begin to tremble, felt herself going liquid with desire. "It's been a long time since I've been with a man, but I don't recall using my ankle much."

He lifted a hand, cupping her cheek. She nestled her face into it, closing her eyes.

"I love you," David murmured. "It seems like I've loved you forever."

She didn't know what to say to him. She couldn't answer him in kind, not yet. She felt for him deeply, but she wasn't ready to call it love. That would be too raw, too real.

Fortunately, he seemed more interested in kissing her than in letting her talk. A moan escaped her as his kiss branded her mouth, sending fire coursing through every small part of her. One of his hands slid down her body, shaping the curve of her waist, the flare of her hip, then moving back up to cover her breast. The soft, kneading motion turned her to water. Hot water. Boiling.

Dealing with David

His other hand slipped behind her back, pressing her hard against him. Her arms went around him, holding him there as if he might disappear. His slim, lean body fitted against her as if it had been meant to be there. She couldn't suppress a brief flash of Rudy, wider and harder in her arms, rougher in his need. There was no comparison. She had always been a little afraid of Rudy at the height of passion. In David's arms, she felt safe.

He broke away suddenly, leaving her gasping. She tried to pull him back, but he arched away from her, taking her face again in his hands.

"There's not enough room on the couch," he said. "I'm afraid I'll hurt you."

She nodded, dazed, totally oblivious to any sensation from her ankle. All she could feel was the aching tingle in her breasts and between her legs. She felt empty, hungry, and only he could fill her.

She protested not at all when he scooped her up and, bending his head to kiss her again, carried her down the hallway to his bedroom. Without taking his mouth from hers, he laid her down on the soft maroon quilt and lowered himself over her.

She opened her legs for him automatically, and he lay down between her still-clad thighs, the hard length of his erection pressing through the jeans to stroke her. His hands pulled her shirt free of her jeans, then slid beneath, caressing her waist, pushing her bra up to stroke her breasts. Tony shrugged at the shirt, wanting it out of the way. David obligingly reached behind her and pulled the shirt over her head, then unfastened her bra. Between the two of them, they got it off her. David pitched it across the room. Tony barely had time to realize it was gone before he ducked his head, closing his mouth over her breast.

Tony's hands burrowed into his hair as his hot mouth suckled one breast, then the other, his tongue leaving a line of fire between them. Every brush of his fingers left a trail of heat behind it, his mouth on her breasts pulling heat through her body. She'd never felt like this before, never had this kind of focused attention paid to her pleasure. For the space of a few breaths, she wondered if she could survive it. The intensity of feeling in her body—the pure, mindless need—was stronger than anything she'd ever felt before.

Her fingers found the buttons on David's shirt and popped them open. He moved his kiss upward, lifting his torso to help her quest. A moment later, she pushed his shirt down to his elbows. He pulled it off the rest of the way.

His body was slim and lean rather than gangly, the muscles defined but not overly heavy. He was built like a swimmer, with broad, cleanly muscled shoulders and a flat stomach bearing a hint of an underlying six-pack. He looked like he worked out enough to stay healthy, but wasn't fanatic about it. Still, his body was strong and masculine, and he smelled like musk and man. She wanted to curl up in that scent and stay there. Kissing the middle of his chest, she let the curly brown hair tickle her lips.

Simultaneously, their hands went for each other's jeans. Tony's reached their destination a split second earlier. David's soft laughter surprised her. She yanked his jeans down, then his briefs, then closed her hand around him.

He moaned and pressed his hips toward her, thrusting his length through the curve of her fist. So hot. So hard.

"I want you," she said.

"Good," he managed, "because you're going to have me."

She let go of him long enough to let him divest her of her jeans; then she embraced him with her legs, pulling him toward her, careful of her ankle but unaware of it at the same time.

He refused her demands, though, instead slipping a hand between them, exploring her heat with his long fingers. She stiffened against him as a deep fire rose. After five years of marriage, she thought she had experienced every level of orgasm, from so-so to intense, but this was already more than she had ever felt before. She heard her own voice from a distance, mouthing incoherencies as the fire twisted around itself within her.

Then came that silent, suspended moment, and the sharp, intense pulsations brought her down. In the midst of it, he plunged inside her.

His hard length speared straight to her womb with a jolt that would have left her breathless had she had breath left. He buried himself in her again and again, his rhythm matching the violent pounding of her heart.

Then he arched above her, his body jerking. She opened her eyes to see his passion—his eyes closed, his dark hair falling damp over his forehead. He seemed to fill her forever; then he relaxed, sagging back down to her, his hands covering her body so that she shook again beneath him.

He rolled away and out of her, too soon. But she was surprised to see the condom on him, which he removed and discarded before rolling back to tuck her against him again.

"When did that happen?" she asked. She hadn't seen him palm it or heard him tear a package open. Much to her chagrin, she hadn't even thought about such practicalities.

He kissed her shoulder. "You *were* distracted for a few minutes there."

She tipped his chin up with a finger and touched his lips. "Next time let me do it."

He smiled and drew her back into his embrace.

Tony thought she dozed for a time; she wasn't sure. In any case, the light outside had darkened a bit when she turned in his arms to see him looking at her.

"What?" She laid her hand on his chest, settling her fingers into the curly brown hair.

He brushed a strand of hair away from her face. "You're beautiful," he said.

Tony smiled. His gentle voice, his touch, the way his long legs wrapped around hers as they lay next to each other—she thought she could live with all of these things for a very long time.

"I'm sorry I got so angry before," she said, caressing the curves of his chest.

He answered by kissing her forehead.

"It's just..."Again, he was there to listen, and she couldn't find the words. "I guess... I guess I'm still carrying a lot of baggage."

"If you need to talk, I'll listen."

She sank into his arms, letting the warmth of his body soak through her. Maybe she could talk to him. Maybe she could finally tell her secrets. She closed her eyes and began to speak, hoping the words would come on their own.

"My marriage was basically a disaster from day one." David shifted, pulling her closer. "We were both too young and too stupid. Especially me." She stopped. Her hands found his arms, holding on to them. She didn't have to tell him everything.

She wanted to.

"I was pregnant when I married Rudy." David said nothing, didn't even move. "I...I lost the baby about a month later. He was good about it at the time, but later..." She stopped again. David's arms tightened around her, very slightly. His breath stirred her hair. "Later he said I lied to him, that I was never really pregnant, and I just told him that to trick him into marrying me. Or once he accused me of sleeping with somebody else, that the baby hadn't been his. I think he resented the marriage itself by then. He'd started cheating on me, and I couldn't do anything to make him happy. He blamed me for all of it. By the time I got smart enough to get out, he had me wondering if I was capable of tying my own shoes."

This time when she stopped, he kissed her hair. "It must have been difficult for you."

"He tried to run my life. I didn't know any better than to let him. I didn't know anything about healthy relationships. I'd never seen one."

"And now?"

"Now I have some idea, from Julia and Jim. But I don't know how to make it happen."

"Don't. Don't *make* it happen. *Let* it happen."

It should have been a profound statement. Unfortunately David's stomach chose that moment to growl quite fiercely. Absorbed in the seriousness of the moment, Tony sputtered a moment before a genuine laugh made it through. David chuckled.

"Maybe we should get something to eat."

David offered to take her out, but Tony decided she didn't want to try it with her ankle still hurting. Instead, they sat on the couch and ate cold cuts while David hunted down esoteric programming on the satellite dish. Finally they settled on a Spanish-language station. David made up his own dialogue, talking over the Spanish-speaking actors. Tony laughed so hard she nearly choked on a gherkin.

"So much for your serious side," she said as her laughter wound down.

"What do you mean?"

She shook her head, still grinning. "Nothing. Just... Julia and I were talking the other day, and she said she thought you were always a little too serious."

David let out a single, sharp bark of a laugh. "It's hard not to be serious when people are beating the crap out of you on a regular basis."

Tony's smile faded. "I'm sorry."

"Why? You never beat me up."

"No, but I wasn't nice to you." She hesitated. "I don't deserve you."

"Nobody deserves me, Tony. I am what they call a Prime Catch."

He would have seemed horribly arrogant if not for the mischievous twinkle in his eyes. She smacked him playfully on the shoulder.

David laughed. "How's the anklc?"

"Better, I guess."

"We should probably put another ice pack on it. Then I can wrap it back up."

David administered appropriate first aid, letting Tony's ankle turn numb while they watched more TV. Afterwards, he reapplied the Ace bandage, his hands gentle.

He was past objective nursing at this point, though. He fastened the bandage, and then his fingers slid up her leg, settling at the bend of her knee. The touch sent heat stirring within her again. Before she quite knew what was happening, he had lifted her down to the floor and was fighting through her clothes to reach her skin.

Heaven came even more quickly this time as he drew her jeans down and, fingers deep inside her, brought her again to orgasm with his mouth. Then he rose to take her, safely sheathed already, kissing her deeply as he joined himself to her. She tasted the dark salt of herself on his tongue, felt him touch the deepest parts of her again and again, until he finished.

With a soft smile, he sank against her, nestling his face in her shoulder.

"You did it again, didn't you?" she said, miffed but not very.

His head popped up. He grinned and rolled away from her, bringing the evidence into view. He had, indeed, applied the condom himself in spite of her earlier request.

"Sorry. I forgot."

She watched him as he walked to the garbage can and back, her smile fading. He looked glorious naked, taut and lean, muscles moving sleekly beneath his skin.

"Are you...?" she ventured. "I mean...maybe we don't actually have to use them?" It was hard to look at him without wanting to cup his erection in her hand, to feel its heat, maybe nibble on it for a while. She wished he'd put some clothes back on.

Then again, maybe not.

Trying not to stare too low, she forced her eyes to his face. "I haven't been with anyone but Rudy. Of course, he was another story, but I settled all that a long time ago. I mean..." It was hard to talk about. "I mean, I got tested. For everything."

David nodded slowly, apparently absorbing what she wasn't saying more than what she was.

"There was a girl in college," he said finally. "I was with her for three years, and for a while I thought she was the One. Then she got a job, and I went on to graduate school." He shrugged. "I'm not really very good with women." Tony had to laugh at that. David returned a lopsided grin. "I'm serious. I never got used to being desirable. And a couple of women walked all over me after I started pulling in some decent money. They seemed to think I should spend it all on them. So, after a while, I came to the conclusion that it wasn't worth it. It had to be the real thing or nothing."

Tony smiled. She felt warm and happy, content in a way she had never been before.

He touched her lips. "You'll stay the night, won't you?"

"Of course I will."

At ten fifteen, David realized that Tony, who had stretched out on the couch and laid her head in his lap, had fallen asleep. She looked quiet, peaceful. He didn't think he'd ever seen her so relaxed and unguarded, unless it had been when she'd fallen apart in his arms. He picked her up and carried her into his room, laying her down on the wide bed. She barely stirred through the operation, sleeping with the deep imperturbability of a child.

When he had tucked her in, he turned the lights off except for the lamp above his computer. As was his habit, he worked for a few hours, finally turning in at two a.m.

He felt guilty for working. It seemed wrong, somehow, that he should make love to the most wonderful woman on the planet, then fiddle away three hours writing up dialogue for

Dark Princes III. But he couldn't go to bed early anymore, and the work had to be done.

When he finally slid into bed, Tony rolled toward him, curling her body into his. He kissed her shoulder, still stunned on some level that she was here in his bed, that she'd decided to stay.

He settled against her warmth, readying his mind for sleep. With the lights doused, it was impossible to see her face, but he saw it in his mind's eye. He wanted the picture to smile, but instead sadness rose in her imagined face.

He hadn't realized how much Rudy had hurt her. He'd never liked Rudy very much, but he'd always assumed that was because of jealousy. Unfortunately for Tony, David's dislike appeared to have been well-founded.

That was in the past, though. From here on out, he would be there for her. He would make sure she never hurt like that again.

And he would start by patching her dreams back together. She'd always wanted to make a living as an artist. The pictures he had given to Rich would make that possible.

David closed his eyes, letting sleep creep over him. Now and forever, as far as he was concerned, Tony, her happiness and her dreams were safe in his keeping.

Chapter Ten

Waking up in David's bed should have been one of the most wonderful moments of Tony's life. Unfortunately, he'd stolen half the blankets and flung half his body over her at some point during the night. She felt like she was being smothered to death on an icy tundra. And David was snoring.

So much for romance. She twisted toward him and poked him in the ribs.

"David?"

He made a horrible choking noise. Tony tried to pick her head up, couldn't, and poked him again. She might be able to push him off if she worked at it, but the angle was awkward.

"David? Wake up. You're squashing me."

He shifted, then jerked back away from her.

"Jeez, I'm sorry." He sat up, pushing a hand through his hair. It stuck straight up along the crown, and the finger-combing didn't help. He looked like a ragamuffin schoolboy, although the dark shadow of morning stubble disrupted the illusion.

Tony sat up next to him, only then noticing that she was still in her clothes. "Sorry I poked you. You're heavy. I thought I might strain something trying to move you." She hesitated, reassessing her surroundings. "Did I fall asleep on the couch?"

"Yeah." David yawned and looked at the clock. It was 8:45, Tony noticed, following his gaze. "You were pretty sacked out. How's the ankle?"

Tony frowned, rotating the joint carefully under the blankets. "Better, I think."

"Good. Let's go jogging."

Tony snorted a laugh. "I don't think so." She rolled toward him, settling her head against his shoulder. "What time did you come to bed?"

"About two."

She peered up at him. "Working?"

"Just tying a few things up. Do you mind?"

Tony smiled slowly, surprised that she found this endearing. "No. No, not at all. Do you mind that I fell asleep on the couch?"

"No." He tapped her on the nose. "Did I tell you I love you?"

She rubbed her hand through the dark, wiry-soft curls on his chest. "Yes. A couple of times, as I recall."

"Did I tell you you're beautiful?"

"I don't remember. But you have my permission to do so."

"You're beautiful," he said, shifting to lay his head between her breasts. "You're beautiful and I love you."

He proceeded to prove it with his mouth and his hands until she moaned under him, straining against the intensity of the sensations he awoke in her. She rode to the crest, paused, then came back down in a release so shattering she thought she heard bells.

"Oh my God," said David, jerking away from her.

Tony's eyes came open, and she gasped at his sudden withdrawal. "What?"

She realized then that she really did hear bells, namely the doorbell.

David rolled sideways off the bed, pausing for a moment in confusion before he reached into the closet for a dark blue silk bathrobe. Tony wasn't sure which she liked better—the sleek, shiny silk or the naked glory beneath it.

"What's going on?" she said, noting that one part of him refused to be covered by the robe, even after he tied the garment shut around his waist.

David looked somewhere between frantic and mortally embarrassed. "It's my mother," he said. "She's here to take me to church. I promised I'd go with her. There's a pancake breakfast today—"

"Maybe you should let her in."

"I don't need to." This pronouncement was followed by the sound of the front door opening, and a voice called David's name. "She has a key," David finished. "I'll be right back."

Alarmed, Tony sat up. "What should I do?"

Pausing with his hand on the doorknob, David looked her over, then smiled. "Mom might prefer it if you put some clothes on."

Self-conscious, Tony gripped the sheet closer against her bare breasts. The clothes she'd slept in lay scattered on the floor next to the bed, the result of David's early morning enthusiasm. "Is she going to freak out?"

"Who, Mom? Not likely. Just...do whatever." He made vague gestures which Tony thought might have something to do with combing her hair. "I'll go talk to her."

"Thanks. But you might want to check little Davey."

Little Davey had deflated a bit, but still poked out between the edges of David's robe. Smiling a sheepish apology, David gave up adjusting things and pulled on a pair of briefs, then headed out.

"Hi, Mom," Tony heard from the hallway, then indistinct voices fading toward the kitchen.

She swung out of bed and gathered her clothes from the floor, dressing quickly before heading into the master bath to run a brush through her hair.

Tony had met Mrs. Peterson before, when she'd come to pick up David after a tutoring session at Tony's house. She'd seemed old to Tony, at least ten years older than her own mother. Suddenly, it felt important that Tony make a good impression. She headed back into the bedroom, then into the hallway, absently pushing her still-wayward hair into place as she walked.

"I'm sorry, Mom," David was saying. "I forgot all about the pancake thing. I might not be able to make it."

"We really need your help." Mrs. Peterson's voice had that chiding tone only a mother could wield effectively. Tony felt instantly guilty, and she wasn't even the one being reprimanded.

"Mom, I just—"

"I don't mind eating some pancakes." Tony rounded the corner into the kitchen. "It's probably too late to make it for church, but we could show up later."

The wide-eyed expression on David's mother's face told Tony he hadn't gotten around to mentioning he had a guest. Tony gave him a narrow-eyed look. David made a slight, shrugging gesture of apology.

"Tony Mullin?" Mrs. Peterson said, regaining some composure. "Is that you?"

"That's right, Mrs. Peterson."

"Oh, call me Maddy."

Tony saw a million questions rise in Maddy's eyes. To her credit, she didn't ask any of them. Instead, she turned to her son, who was a good foot taller than she, and smacked him across the shoulder.

"You didn't tell me you had company, David. Why you can't be honest with me, I don't know. You're twenty-seven years old—you'd think you'd have more respect for your own mother."

"I was getting ready to," David mumbled, while Tony suppressed a laugh.

"It's really okay, Mrs. Peterson—Maddy. I'd really like to go to the breakfast. What time does it start?"

"Eleven o'clock," said Maddy. "It's really a brunch, but why quibble?"

"I volunteered to cook," David said, obviously protesting. "So it really wouldn't be that much fun."

"Sure it would. And if you weasel out, I'll lose all respect for you."

Maddy gave a triumphant grin. "Good." She looked at her watch. "I'd love to stay and get acquainted, Tony, but David's father is waiting patiently in the car. I'll see you two at ten thirty."

David saw his mother off while Tony meandered into the kitchen, looking for the coffeemaker. She had found it, filled the pot with water and was looking for the coffee when David joined her.

"It's really okay with you if we go?" he said. He moved up behind her, settling his hands on her shoulders.

"It's fine," she said. She turned in his arms, facing him. "It'll be...domestic."

Dealing with David

David reached up to open a cabinet and pull out the coffee. "I'm glad we slept late, though. I don't think I would have been very comfortable sitting next to my mother in church after fornicating all night."

Tony cocked an eyebrow at him, then saw he was grinning.

"Why? Do you think what we did was wrong?"

"No." He set down the coffee to nestle his hands around her waist. "The way I feel about you, I think it was about the rightest thing I've ever done in my life." He leaned forward to kiss her, tender, one hand closing gently over the curve of her breast.

Tony blinked back sudden tears. Forcing lightness into her tone, she said, "We've got forty-five minutes. We can do it again before we leave."

He grinned, but there was a softness in his eyes, and he let his fingers brush lightly along the curve of her cheek. "I like that plan."

The events of the early afternoon left Tony with a great deal to think about on her long drive home.

The first thing she'd noticed was that David had a remarkable rapport with his parents. Tony envied him that. Tony hadn't really known her father very well. He'd left his family when Tony was six and hadn't made much effort to keep in touch. Tony's relationship with her mother had always been stormy, and although they'd settled on an amicable truce a few years ago, Tony knew she and her mother would never be friends.

Tony also envied the skill with which David created pancakes. Obviously, he wasn't one of those bachelors who depended on McDonald's for sustenance. Tony, on the other hand, had never learned to cook anything more complicated than Hamburger Helper.

The third thing she'd noticed was that David really *wasn't* good with women. A few truly lovely young ladies had approached him, blatantly looking for more than a couple of flapjacks. David stammered and flushed and retreated to Tony's side.

So why was he so suave and comfortable with her? It made no sense to Tony, but she found it flattering.

It wasn't until she had pulled into a parking space in front of her apartment building that Tony realized she hadn't thought of Rudy—not once—in at least twenty-four hours.

All in all, that was definitely a good thing.

Tony woke Monday morning, sweaty and damp, to the sound of her radio. She'd been dreaming about David. If he'd been in bed next to her, she would have been late for work.

As it was, she arrived early, unable to hold back a smile and a bounce in her step which had to annoy her current coworkers, especially since it was Monday.

"Good weekend?" the department supervisor asked as Tony came whistling into the office. They'd hit it off well when Tony had started the assignment. It felt like a place she might be able to stay for a while.

"Great weekend," Tony confirmed.

"Care to elaborate?"

"No, not really, but thanks for asking."

A pile of work already waited in Tony's in-basket. She booted up her computer and started working.

The morning hours seemed to fly by. Tony couldn't recall a time when she had been this happy.

Julia had been right. Tony *did* need someone like David. Someone who would prop her up, not tear her down. Someone open, up front and honest. Someone who would let her live her own life, not try to control her. Nothing in the past mattered anymore. Not Rudy, not the old David. Not the old Tony, either. The last few weeks had felt like coming out of a gloomy winter day into the promise of spring. Until the sun had started to move in, she hadn't realized she was in the dark.

Talking on the phone to a client, she began to doodle. Maybe she could start painting again. David had money, after all. She could quit her job, quit her classes, maybe do whatever she wanted if she married him—

She cut the thought off, so surprised by it that she almost didn't hear what the person on the phone had said to her. Rooting her brain to the present, she finished the phone message, hung up and returned to her computer.

Marry David? That was moving too fast, wasn't it? She had rushed into one marriage, and she didn't want to do it again. Especially not when her motives were so questionable. Thinking like that was too much like what Rudy had accused her of—wanting into David's wallet.

There was no denying she had feelings for him, though. No denying she liked the idea of waking up in the morning with him next to her. Besides, could it really be called rushing when you'd known someone for fourteen years?

Yes, it could, she decided. The man she'd met two weeks ago at the reunion wasn't the same David Peterson she'd known in high school. And even back then, she hadn't known him that well. There were a hundred, a thousand things about him she didn't know.

Tony smiled to herself. She would take the time to learn all of them, and she would enjoy every minute of it.

At ten thirty, the office phone rang. Tony noticed the sound because it was the double ring of an outside line, and most of the calls came from in-house. She was at the copier, though, around the corner from her desk. Someone else picked it up. Tony gathered her completed pile of copies and went back to her desk to stuff them into envelopes.

"Tony?" Cathy was holding the phone away from her ear, hand securely over the mouthpiece. "I think this is for you."

Tony frowned. "You *think* it's for me?"

"It's somebody named Rich at Tachyon Software."

Tony's frown deepened. It took her a moment to place the name. Why would David's partner be calling her? Had something happened to David?

"I'll take it." She took a seat at her desk and took a quick breath before picking up the phone.

"Antonytte Mullin."

The voice that answered was bright and cheerful. "Hi, Ms. Mullin. This is Rich McKay from Tachyon Software. My partner, David Peterson, gave me your name and number along with some drawings you did."

"Drawings?" She felt like her head was completely empty. Then a memory floated by: sitting awake in David's guest room, drawing fanciful sketches of women in chain mail.

She'd left the pictures at his house. He'd found them and given them to his partner. Without so much as mentioning it to Tony.

The bottom of her stomach dropped out. She felt ill. What the hell did he think he was doing?

Rich went on, his voice sparkling. "Yes. The pictures are a little rough, but I've shared them with our design team, and we all agree that you've captured the essence of the *Dark Princes III* characters perfectly. I'd like to set up an interview with you to discuss our options. There's been some talk of hiring you on as a graphic artist. Toward that end, I'd like to run a few things by you—"

"Graphic artist?" Tony barely heard her own voice. Her ears were ringing.

"Yes." Rich hesitated. "Ms. Mullin, is there a problem?"

Tony swallowed. She wondered if the fact she knew nothing about being a videogame artist, had no experience in the area, and didn't even know she'd been submitted for the position constituted a problem. Surely there was some mistake. Or was David using his position in the company to shoehorn her into a job. God, that would just be—

She forced that thought to break off and swallowed again. "This is just...unexpected."

"Really? I got the impression David had already spoken to you."

"No. No, not really." Tony gathered herself. That didn't sound good at all. What was going on? Why had David done this without telling her? He probably thought he was doing her a favor, but God... This was *her* life. It had to be *her* choice. She couldn't go down this path again.

Still. Artist. She took a steadying breath. "Mr. McKay, I'm going to have to finagle something with my schedule. Can you give me some idea when you might be free?"

Rich named several dates and times, and Tony penciled them in on her calendar. The haze had returned, along with an unreasoning terror that grew huge in her chest. She could barely speak to close her conversation with Rich. It all felt surreal. She just didn't know enough about what was going on, and the image of David as a puppet master, with her attached to a series of marionette strings, wouldn't leave her head.

When they had finished, she clicked off the connection and ran for the ladies' room. There she locked herself in a stall and turned her back to the door. She banged her head against it a couple of times to keep from crying. It didn't work.

She couldn't believe he'd done this. Surely, normal people didn't conduct business this way. You didn't just take somebody's casual sketches and present them to your art director as a professional portfolio. How the hell had David managed to be so successful if that was the way he ran things?

And what the *hell* was she thinking, considering taking the interview? She had no experience, no résumé, no formal portfolio—they couldn't do anything but eat her alive. It was just another chance for Tony to be humiliated, to have her dreams spat back in her face.

But David wouldn't do that to her, would he? He wouldn't set her up for failure. But would he make his partner give her a job in spite of her lack of experience? That might be even worse.

Finally, she gave up and let herself cry. She didn't know if the tears came from anger or despair.

She heard the restroom door open, then, "Tony?" That was Cathy's voice. "Tony, are you all right?"

Tony leaned her head back against the stall door. "I don't know." She pulled some toilet paper from the roll and dabbed her eyes. The tissue came back black with mascara. She blew her nose, then unlocked the stall and came out.

The big mirror above the sinks told her everything she didn't want to know. She looked like a raccoon, eye shadow and mascara smeared under her eyes.

Cathy looked at her, concern heavy on her face. "Who was that on the phone?"

Undoubtedly, Cathy was certain by now that someone had died.

"It was somebody who wanted to talk to me about a job."

And that, of course, sounded absolutely ludicrous. Cathy's concern changed to puzzlement.

"I don't understand. Shouldn't that make you happy?"

"It probably would under other circumstances." Tony pulled a paper towel from the dispenser on the wall and wet it in the sink. Her eye makeup looked hopeless, but she could at least try to clean herself up. "I had no idea I had applied."

Cathy shook her head. "Obviously, your life is more complicated than mine." She smiled and moved back toward the door. "I'll cover for you for a while, if you need me to."

Tony nodded. "Thanks."

The eye makeup was hopeless. There was nothing left for it but to wash it off. Tony didn't carry makeup with her, though, except for a tube of lipstick, so she'd just have to do without for the rest of the day.

Wiping smears of eye shadow from her face, she wondered. Was she nuts? She'd never, ever dreamed that someone might offer her a position as an art director at a major software company. It could almost be a dream come true.

Then again, she really had no idea what a graphic artist at a video game company would *do*, aside from the obvious. No company in their right mind would hire a completely inexperienced person for such an obviously important job. The only explanation that made any sense to her was that David had strong-armed Rich into considering her. He'd done what he thought would be best for her, without consulting her, and had used his influence to do it instead of letting her find her way on her own merits. It was infuriating. It was Rudy all over again, except upside down and backward, which made it even worse, because she knew he had no idea she'd see it as controlling.

But it was.

Anger flared, making her mouth tighten to a thin line against her teeth. David had gone behind her back, done what *he* thought was right for her without even bothering to ask her first.

David had a great deal of explaining to do.

Tony was marginally calmer when she walked back out to her desk.

Cathy gave her a wave. "Feeling better?"

Tony sat down. "Maybe. Now I'm just freaking out." She folded her hands on her desk, considering. "Can I take a few minutes to go outside and make a phone call? Do you mind?"

"No, go right ahead."

Tony retreated outside into the parking lot, well out of earshot of anyone who might come out for a smoke break. There was a picnic table near the edge of the lot, where people sometimes came to eat lunch. The table faced west, toward the mountains. Some of the higher peaks were visible from here, still sheathed in white. The sight calmed her—the mountains always did. Even if her life fell completely apart, they would always be there.

Courage gathered, anger settled in the pit of her stomach where she could hopefully control it, Tony took a seat and dialed David's office.

His secretary, Nancy, answered.

"Hi," said Tony. "This is Tony Mullin. Is David in?"

"Just a minute. I'll check." Nancy sounded young, pretty and perky. Much like the dental hygienist Tony had found with Rudy. Anger lifted a tendril into her throat.

Stop it. There was no point dredging up the past. Or the future, for that matter, as she suddenly pictured herself finding David in a similarly compromising situation.

He wouldn't do that.

He's trying to control you, just like Rudy did. She felt like she was in one of those old cartoons, with a devil on one shoulder condemning David and an angel on the other defending him.

He thinks he's giving you a chance to follow your dream.

He thinks he can do whatever he wants, and you should be happy about it because he's a man.

He loves you.

That was what he'd said, anyway. Tony put her face in her hands, pressing the tips of her fingers against her eyelids. Bright red flowers blossomed in the dark behind her closed lids. Why hadn't he at least talked to her about it first? Let her make her own decision—

The hold music on the line suddenly clicked off, followed by David's voice. He, too, sounded overly perky. Tony ground her teeth, fighting back the automatic surge of emotion at the sound of his voice. She needed to be centered to have this conversation. She couldn't think about his motives, or, worse, about how it reminded her of her previous life. She had to let all that go.

God, it was hard. There was just no way to be objective about this.

"Hey, Tony! What's up?"

Tony hesitated, making certain her voice would be under control before she spoke. "I got a call from Rich this morning."

"Oh, great! When's the interview?"

Tony let her eyes pop back open. The red blossoms from the press of her fingers continued to float in her vision. "I didn't schedule an interview."

There was a long silence. "Why not?"

Oh my God. Was he really this obtuse? It might have been endearing had the situation not been so fraught with...well, everything. As it was, Tony had a sudden urge to crawl through the phone and strangle him.

"If someone called you out of the blue and asked you to schedule an interview for a job you had no idea existed and you hadn't even applied for, what would you do?"

Another silence, this one shorter. "You would kick ass at this job, Tony."

"How? How in the world would I kick ass at this job? I've never worked as a graphic artist. I know nothing about video games. I just draw a little, and sketch and paint sometimes."

"You're really selling yourself short—"

"David, it's my life. I get to decide what I want to do. If I go in for that interview, I'm going to look like an idiot."

Yet another silence. "You're angry?"

Was she angry? Yeah, she decided, maybe she was. "You had no right to do this, David. Did you even think about talking to me first?"

"Well—" He stopped, as if expecting her to interrupt him again. This time she let him talk. "I did, but I figured you'd just say no."

"With good reason." Now she was angry. "I have no experience, no formal training—seriously, David, what the hell?"

"I just—"

The anger shifted inside her, becoming something darker, a little more like despair. "You and I both know that if I got this job, it would be because you made it happen, not because I'm the best candidate—or even remotely qualified, for that matter. I can't do that. I can't."

"Tony—"

She hung up before he could finish.

She sat quietly for a moment, letting the spring sun warmed her. The phone rang and vibrated in her hand. It was David, calling back. She pressed the "reject call" button.

So this was it. It was over. He'd never speak to her again after this. She wasn't sure she wanted him to. She should be sad, have a nice little breakdown, but she couldn't. She was too numb.

Quietly, she walked back into the building and returned to work.

A few miles away, David hung up his own phone, folded his hands together and propped his chin on them.

This was an unexpected development. She was supposed to have been surprised and pleased. She was supposed to have scheduled the interview right away, accepted the job and been blissfully happy.

How could he have been so far off the mark? He should have known she'd react poorly if he took things into his own hands. But he'd known she'd never take the step on her own.

Which was her choice. Or it should've been.

He scrubbed his face with his hands, angry with himself. It had seemed like a good idea at the time, but that had been before he'd gotten to know her better, and before he'd heard her explanation of why she and Rudy had broken up.

Before they'd slept together.

"Way to go, David," he muttered. "Way to screw that one up nine ways to Sunday."

He should have listened to that little voice in his head when he'd had the chance. And now he had no idea how he could fix what he'd done.

He clicked his phone back on and called his mother.

By the time she got home that evening, Tony's anger had mutated into a bitter emptiness. She should have known better than to trust a man again. Something about her must just attract men who wanted to rule her life.

She threw something frozen into the microwave and cooked it, then sat at the table and ate it while she watched the evening news. She had an urge to call Julia but shook it off. She'd just sound stupid now, after confiding her high hopes.

Depression setting in, she found a half bag of chocolate chips in the back of the cabinet and collapsed onto the couch to munch on them. After a few minutes, she tossed them aside. Apparently, a couple months of sitting in an open bag had leached out all their chocolateness, because they weren't making her feel any better.

Just then, the doorbell rang. Tony groaned. It was probably some kid selling Girl Scout cookies, or candy bars for the pep squad fundraiser or something. The mood she was in now, she'd buy a whole case.

She dragged the door open to face not a gap-toothed girl in a baggy green uniform, but a tall, lanky man hiding behind a veritable bush of red and white roses.

"Hi, Tony—"

She slammed the door.

He knocked this time. Tony returned to the couch and turned up the volume on the TV.

He knocked again, this time in an annoying, persistent rhythm. Dum da da da DUM da da da DUM da da da DUM...

And then he began to sing. At the top of his lungs. Imitating Elvis and not doing a very good job.

She tried plugging her ears, but he wailed enthusiastically about fools rushing in. When he got to, "I can't help..." she ran to the door to keep him from uttering the last five words.

"All right, all right," she said. "If you'll stop singing, you can come in."

He came in, handing her the mass of flowers. Tony couldn't remember ever having seen so many roses outside a flower shop.

"They're lovely," she said, trying not to sound touched. She took them, albeit reluctantly, and gestured toward the couch. "Have a seat."

"Do you want your chocolate?" He held up a gilt box. "It's Godiva."

She snatched it from his hand. He was making it really, really hard to stay mad at him.

"Fine."

She carried the gifts into the kitchen, found a vase and arranged the flowers. Then she looked at the box of chocolates.

She should leave it unopened. That way when she threw him out, she could throw the box after him.

Forget it. It was Godiva.

She opened the box, took out a piece and let it melt on her tongue. Now *there* was some chocolate with chocolateness intact.

To David's credit, he said nothing at all throughout this operation. When Tony returned to the living room, he was sitting quietly on the couch, hands folded in his lap. He looked like a little boy who'd been sent to the corner for a timeout. A shock of hair hung over his eyes as he stared down at his folded hands. A small, vertical line had formed between his brows.

She was feeling a bit softer toward him now. Chocolate was good for that kind of thing. Still, she slid into the recliner, putting as much space between them as she could, hoping it would help her maintain her objectivity.

"Thanks for letting me in," he said.

"I was afraid one of the neighbors might think you were a cat in heat and shoot you."

"Tony, I'm sorry." He leaned forward, his expression earnest. She crossed her arms over her chest, still trying to maintain that space. It was getting harder.

"I had no right to do what I did with the pictures. It's just—when I saw them, I knew they were exactly what I was looking for. But I didn't know for sure if I could work it all out with Rich and the other artists, so I didn't say anything to you right away. I didn't want you to get your hopes up."

"I'm a big girl, David. I can deal with disappointment." Trouble was, she'd gained too much of that ability through firsthand experience. "Look, if you like the pictures so much, why don't I just sell them to you outright? It makes a lot more sense than endangering your new project with a completely inexperienced artist."

"I can't just scan the pictures and pass them on to another artist. The spark would get lost in the translation, and we need to maintain continuity with the other characters."

"So you've got things set up with Rich so he'll just say hey, okay, no problem, have a job, because after all, you're the boss's girlfriend." She stopped, tears springing from nowhere. She blinked them back, thankful he stayed silent long enough for her to compose herself. "That's not fair to me, it's not fair to you, and it's not fair to Rich. Especially since I'm not even your girlfriend."

David's face went strangely white, in patches under his eyes. "Tony...don't do this."

Tony sagged in her chair, frustration boiling in her stomach. "You really don't get it, do you? I got out of my marriage because my husband did things behind my back and told me how I should live my life. Now what are you doing? You're doing things behind my back and telling me how to live my life. I thought you were different. I thought you'd let me be me. But..." This was what she'd been afraid of. That she'd moved too fast, taken everything at face value. Let herself hope. Now she had no choice but to kill that hope as quickly and thoroughly as she could. "If this is the way it's going to be, if this is your idea of being supportive—I can't do that. I need to make my own decisions. I need control. I don't need you engineering things to 'fix' my life." She made air quotes, and he leaned away from her in the chair, his expression devastated. He rubbed his face hard with one hand, then leaned forward again.

"Don't let this go just because I screwed up. Don't let your dream job get away just because I made a bad choice. Can you promise me that, at least?"

She bit the inside of her lip to keep from sobbing. "I don't know, David. I just don't know."

He stood slowly, his expression one of heart-wrenching sadness.

"I wish you would do one thing, Tony. Not for me. For yourself."

"What?"

"Talk to Rich. See what he can offer you."

Tony shook her head. "You'd be nuts to hire me. I don't know anything about software development."

David walked to the door. "You never know until you try."

As he closed the door behind him, it struck her that he'd asked her not to give up on the job. He hadn't said anything about salvaging their relationship. And she didn't know what to make of that at all.

Chapter Eleven

His words haunted her all night. She kept picturing her name in the credits of *Dark Princes III*—that part of the game nobody ever looked at. She pictured herself spending the day drawing elves and orcs and Aethelfried in chain mail.

Well, she was certain there would be more to it than that, but it had to be better than accounting.

At breakfast, she played with her cereal until it got soggy, then poured it down the sink and toasted a bagel instead.

You never know until you try.

A part of her, a tiny part that she had quelled a long time ago, wanted to schedule the interview just to find out if she had any chance at all. But that would mean taking risks, turning her back on the practical nature she'd been trying to nurture since her divorce.

It would mean trusting David.

It might even mean working for David. And she didn't want to get the job just because of her relationship with the company's co-owner. She couldn't get her brain past that thought—that Rich really didn't want Tony on the team, but David had insisted he talk to her.

But David had said he really liked the pictures. Surely he wouldn't endanger his game over her.

Tony threw her half-eaten bagel down in disgust.

"You are waffling big-time," she told herself. Somehow it seemed she had to hash this out aloud, just to get it to make sense. "One minute you're accusing him of using you to get the pictures, the next minute you're thinking he'd railroad you into the company because you're his..." His what? His girlfriend? His lover? They hadn't even been together long enough to work *that* out.

"Good grief."

She pulled a raisin out of her bagel and chewed thoughtfully. She'd already been stewing so long she was going to be late for work. But it had to be worked out.

"Okay." Talking aloud seemed to be helping her focus. "Forget David. Pretend he has nothing to do with this. Do you *want* to try for this job?"

She sat for a minute or two, waiting for an answer. Finally it came to her, bubbling up from the back of her mind through a quagmire of doubt and the long-term suppression of her dreams.

"Yes."

Rich was able to see her that morning. In fact, he seemed eager to have her come in. She apologized for not calling the day before and scheduled the interview for ten thirty. Then she called in sick to the temp agency.

Dressed in a lightweight wool suit she'd made herself, Tony drove to the Tachyon building. She almost expected to see David, but Rich met her in the lobby. Sandy-haired, looking more like a surfer than a computer programmer and wearing a Bugs Bunny tie that looked like something out of David's collection, Rich put her quickly at ease with his informal manner and obvious enthusiasm for his work.

"So," Rich said as they rode the elevator to the third floor, "you went to high school with David?"

"That's right."

Rich nodded. "Lucky he ran into you at the wedding thing. Whatever the hell that was."

Tony schooled her features, wondering what else David had told him. "Yes, I suppose it is."

Rich held the door open for her; then they walked down a short hallway. Two large wooden doors stood side by side in an alcove at the end of it. Between them, an attractive blonde woman spoke on the phone in crisp, professional tones. Tony recognized the voice. This was Nancy, then, David's secretary and apparently Rich's as well. Looking up, Tony saw that one of the doors had David's name on it. The other said Richard McKay.

Rich winked at Nancy, who fluttered a wave in return without losing stride in her conversation. She was attractive, appeared to be competent, and didn't look anything like a dental hygienist. *Let it go, Tony.* She could, she decided. She really could.

Rich's office wasn't particularly sumptuous, but the slightly worn leather couch facing the big walnut desk looked comfortable. Rich gestured to it, and Tony sat down, laying her briefcase on her lap.

"So," said Rich. He settled behind the big desk. "Down to business. Résumé?"

Tony handed it over with some trepidation. Rich began to read, and a slowly growing frown told her she'd been right to be concerned.

After a time, he laid the résumé down and looked at her.

"I was under the impression you had more directly related experience."

Tony's stomach dropped. She didn't know if she was disappointed or relieved.

"I'm sorry if David told you that."

Rich shrugged. "David didn't tell me anything at all." He grinned. "Hell, I didn't even know if you were a man or a woman until I called you."

Tony realized her mouth was hanging open and snapped it shut.

"I guess he didn't want to prejudice my decision." Rich leaned back in his chair, lacing his fingers together in front of him. "I must say he's left me with an interesting dilemma."

"I..." Tony trailed off, took a breath and tried again. "I was under the impression David would have some input on the final decision."

"Nope. Not a bit. As of yesterday, he's no longer on the *Dark Princes III* team. He's fully committed to *Tommy Turtle Learns His Manners*, a graphic adventure set in the Land of the Messy Mudskippers. For ages three to seven." He hesitated, a smile lurking around his mouth. "This all surprises you, doesn't it?"

Tony wanted to laugh, but it didn't seem quite appropriate, even given the ludicrous situation.

"Frankly, Rich," she said, trying not to sound impertinent, "I didn't even know my artwork was being considered until you called me. They're not even formal drawings. They're just something I sketched at David's house when he was kind enough to put me up during a snowstorm."

Rich shook his head, bemused. "He didn't tell you he'd sent them to me?"

"No."

"Well, that's David for you. For such an intelligent guy, he can be a complete lamebrain sometimes."

This time Tony couldn't suppress the laugh.

"I suppose this puts a whole new slant on things, doesn't it?" she said.

"Yes, it does." He leaned forward. "But you know what? I think we can work it out."

When Tony came home, she had six messages on her voice mail. Wondering who could have possibly called her, she played them back.

The first was Stevie Wonder singing, "I Just Called to Say I Love You." The song played straight through until the voice mail cut it off. Then came "Longer" by Dan Fogelberg, then four more hopelessly mushy songs.

"David Peterson," Tony muttered, listening to "You're My Home," by Billy Joel. "If I didn't love you so much, I'd hate your guts." At least it was classic rock. If he'd sent her any pop songs from the current top forty, she might have sworn off men forever.

When the last song had ended, she picked up the phone and called his house.

"You know," she said when he answered, "all those songs are lovely, but you didn't leave a number."

"How'd it go?" he asked.

Tony hesitated. Was he asking out of concern for her or because he wanted to be sure he'd gotten his way? *Be honest. He's not a self-centered asshole, remember?* Her poor little interior voice was going to wear herself out at this rate, as much encouragement as Tony needed.

"It went well, I think."

"Are you happy?"

Tony smiled. At least he'd asked the right question. "Yes. Very."

He hesitated only a moment before asking the next question.

"Would you be too terribly opposed to dinner? On me? To celebrate?"

"Not too terribly." She glanced at her watch. It would take nearly an hour for her to drive to Eagle Creek...

"I'll be there in twenty minutes."

"What? I thought you were at home."

"I'm at the office. I'm having calls to my house forwarded. And in case you're wondering, no, I haven't talked to Rich. He had a hot date and left before I got here."

Tony shook her head. He could be so dense, yet so sweet. "All right. I'll see you in a few minutes, then."

He came bearing gifts again, this time a bottle of champagne and brand-new crystal champagne flutes. He had on a sweater that accentuated the broadness of his shoulders. There was an oddly strained look to his face that he seemed to be working hard to hide.

She'd thought she would still be mad at him. She wasn't. She wanted to kiss him but restrained herself. They needed a bit of time first.

He gave her a comically anxious look. "I don't have to sing this time, do I?"

Tony flushed. "No, that won't be necessary. Come on in."

David crossed into the kitchen and set the champagne and glasses on the counter. Tony followed him, watching, waiting for the inevitable question.

He turned, leaning against the counter. "So what exactly are we celebrating?"

Tony lifted her chin, studying him while she considered her answer.

"What if I told you I didn't take the job?"

He nodded, some surprise in his eyes but no disappointment. "Then we celebrate that you got far enough to be considered."

"What if Rich didn't even offer it to me?"

"Then...you were brave enough to take the interview. That's a big step, you know."

Tony nodded. She crossed her arms over her chest, weighing her next question.

"And what if I didn't let Rich keep the pictures?"

Something flashed in David's eyes, but Tony couldn't tell what it was. Surprise, certainly, but what else? Disappointment?

He shook his head. "You know, it doesn't matter. It really doesn't matter." He stepped toward her, settling his hands against her waist. "I love you, Tony. I can find another artist, but I'll never find another you. If I ever implied that those drawings were more important to me than you, then I was stupid."

Tony looked up at him, tingling with desire, wishing he'd kiss her. But there was still more to say.

"It was wrong of you to send those pictures," she said, "but in a way I'm glad you did."

He lifted his eyebrows, waiting. His long thighs nestled against hers, warm and strong. Yes, she wished he'd kiss her. And then she wished he'd carry her into her bedroom and make love to her until she passed out.

"It made me take a serious look at my life," she went on. "And I realized I've been hiding from myself. I've been chasing this accounting degree, and it's not what I want at all. When I went in today, I assumed Rich knew that I had no experience, and that you and I were more than casual acquaintances. But since you hadn't told him anything, we were able to look at the situation logically and come to a compromise."

"I'm glad it worked out so that you're happy with it."

"I *am* happy." She paused, drawing out the moment. "Rich is going to buy the pictures from me, along with any others I do for *Dark Princes III*. And he's agreed to take me on in a paid internship so I can learn the business from the inside. At the same time, he's going to pay for me to take classes so I can get a degree in graphic arts. Then, when my internship is over, he says he'll move me into a position as an artist or maybe even art director on another project."

David absorbed this, nodding soberly. "It's a good solution. I'm not sure I would have thought of it."

Tony couldn't hold back her enthusiasm anymore. "Oh, I think it's going to be great, David. The pay's not fantastic, but it's better than what I make temping, and it'll be really nice to have a steady job." She stopped, realizing she was gushing. David was grinning that big, goofy, adolescent grin.

"What?" Tony demanded.

"It's just great seeing you so happy."

She shifted away from him. "Hold on. You're not out of the woods yet."

The grin didn't fade. "You mean you haven't forgiven me yet?"

One side of her mouth pulled up. "I'm working on it."

David sank to his knees, looking up at her. "What must I do, my lady, to earn your forgiveness?"

"First, I want you to promise to discuss with me beforehand any decisions which directly affect me."

David nodded. "Fair enough. Do you need to hear about Tommy Turtle?"

"Actually, I'd rather not. But if you find Messy Mudskipper sketches lying around, you might want to ask me before you take them to the office."

"Not a problem. You might have to remind me, though. I can be—well, overly focused about my work."

"So I've noticed."

"And are there any other demands?"

"I want you to take me to dinner. Somewhere classy and expensive. Then I want to come back here, and I want you to make love to me until I tell you to stop." She glanced at her watch. "Which probably won't be until some time late Thursday."

"Gladly. Anything else?"

Tony made a great show of considering. "No, I don't think so."

David came to his feet and took her in his arms, drawing her close against him. Then he lowered his head and kissed her.

He was warm and sweet but as hard as she needed him to be, possessing her with his kiss, yet freeing her at the same time. It was as deep and pure and true as anything she had ever known.

After a long time, he drew away.

"On second thought," Tony said, "let's skip dinner."

About the Author

Katriena Knights wrote her first poem when she was three years old and had to dictate it to her mother under the bathroom door (her timing has never been very good). Now she's the author of several paranormal and contemporary romances. She grew up in a miniscule town in Illinois and now lives in a miniscule town in Colorado with her two children, her goofy dog, two ferrets and a weird little gerbil. Visit her at her website at http://katrienaknights.com, or at her blog at http://katrienaknights.blogspot.com.

The road to heartbreak is paved with honorable intentions...

Fever Cure
© 2011 Phillipa Ashley

After a year dealing with her mum's health scare and the end of a bad relationship, Keira Grayson was looking forward to kicking up her heels at her best friend's wedding. Until she kicks off her (spare) knickers in front of the trifecta of perfection. Tom Carew. Son of an earl, honorable doctor and possibly the hottest man on the planet.

One look at Keira's delightful embarrassment, and Tom's hormone meter spins off the charts. Trouble is, his bags are already packed to return to the jungles of Papua New Guinea. He has patients waiting—and amends to make for a terrible choice that left devastation in its wake.

They both reason that indulging in a one-time dinner date won't hurt…until their inhibitions melt away in the heat of their lethal sexual chemistry. Leaving Keira wondering if a sizzling fling is just what the doctor ordered, or another prescription for relationship disaster. And Tom fighting a battle against inner demons that could shatter both their hearts.

Warning: This book contains a hot aristocratic doctor, sparky heroine, new uses for a chaise longue, a steamy shower scene and a knicker-ripping encounter in a four-poster bed.

Available now in ebook and print from Samhain Publishing.

www.samhainpublishing.com

*Green for the planet.
Great for your wallet.*

Romance

HORROR

www.samhainpublishing.com

CPSIA information can be obtained at www.ICGtesting.com
Printed in the USA
BVOW012240200213

313841BV00002B/81/P